CONFESSING MY LOVE TO A HUSTLER

TYANNA & NIKKI RAE

Confessing My Love to a Hustler

Confessing MY LOVE TO A Hustler

TYANNA & NIKKI RAE

SYNOPSIS

Married since high school, Zyla Holmes is no longer experiencing wedded bliss. The allure of her shotgun-marriage to Mark, once the love of her life, has faded. Mark takes her for granted and expects her to submit to any and everything he desires. Zyla has had enough of dealing with his drama.

Mark Holmes loves his wife, Zyla, but he doesn't love their traditional married life. He figures that if their marriage was open, Zyla wouldn't constantly fuss at him for cheating and hanging out. When Zyla rejects his idea, Mark continues to do him while still holding selfishly to his marriage.

With more money than he knew what to do with, Jaxen "Jax" Taylor feels like it's finally time for him to get up out of the hood. He moves to the suburbs and lives a nice, quiet life... except for when he hears his neighbors, Zyla and Mark, out front arguing. During one of their disputes, Jax locks eyes with Zyla. After that first encounter, he can't get her out of his mind.

Zyla is struck the same way by her sexy neighbor, but she has a marriage to consider. Will her unhappy union lead her into Jax's arms or will she try to save her failing relationship with her husband?

MARK

I was lying on my back trying to figure out the lie I was about to tell my wife once again. I knew the late night at the office shit was starting to get old, but hell, I didn't wanna switch the lie up. Then she would probably start to think something. The feeling of something plastic, cold, and wet on my chest caused me to jump up.

"Man! Kia, what the fuck!" I snapped, jumping up.

"It's time for you to get the fuck up and go home to your family anyway. I just thought I would literally hit you with the news before you go," Kia sassed.

Kia was some chick that I had been fucking with on and off for five months. Whenever I was ready to leave to go home, she would get in her moods, knowing I was a married man before I even got here. Yeah, I always let any bitch I fuck with, know I was married, and wasn't leaving my wife. So, it was their choice to continue to deal with me.

"Why do you always get like that when I'm ready to leave?"

"Mark, let's not start with all the questions. Did you even pay attention to what I threw at you?" I looked down on the bed, noticed a pregnancy test lying there, and it was indeed positive. I looked at Kia with a mean mug.

"Yo' you really just hit me with a pissy ass pregnancy test? You straight nasty for that dumb shit."

"Nigga, I just showed you that I was pregnant, and that's all you worried about is me hitting you with the test? How about what we gone do about this shit?"

"What you mean? You know I can't have no baby by you, ma."

"Oh, you can't have no baby by me, but you can keep fucking me raw? Mark, get the fuck out of my house. I'ma give you a couple of days to decide how we about to work this out, because I didn't make this baby alone."

"Kia, you don't even know if that's my fucking baby. I know you ain't only fucking me, so you better go ahead and find one of them other dudes to pin this baby on. I'm out and you don't have to worry about me coming the fuck back," I said while getting up and throwing my clothes on.

"You know what, Mark? You've messed with the wrong heart. If you don't get with me in a couple of days, I'll be contacting the Misses."

"Kia, I don't give a fuck what you do. All I know is that's not gone make me say we gone be a happy family. If you know like I know, you will get rid of that baby. You don't have any money to take care of it anyway." I turned my attention away from her then made my way into the bathroom to wash my face. I wasn't about to play with Kia and her crazy ass. She thinks if she threatens me with telling my wife, I'll give in. After putting my clothes on and getting my shit together, I walked back into the bedroom. Kia was sitting on the bed crying. I didn't care though. Her ass should have made sure she was on birth control or using protection.

"I'm out, ma. If you decide to get rid of the baby, let me know. If not, you better start calling them other niggas," I bluntly said before walking out of the door. I knew that shit was cold what I just said, but these chicks be on some other shit. Once I got to the car, I powered on my phone, and all these missed calls, voice mails, and text messages started coming up.

Babe: Mark, where are you?
Babe: I had to take Zoey to the hospital.
Babe: I've been calling you all night.
Babe: I guess you had more important shit to do. We home now they finally got her fever to break.

After looking at all my wife's messages, I completely felt like shit. I couldn't believe she had to sit in the hospital all night with my baby and I was laid up with a bitch. I couldn't do shit but shake my fucking head. I pulled out my phone and dialed my partner Josh's number. The phone rung three times until he finally picked up.

"I'm so tired of covering up for your stupid ass. You be having my wife side-eying me and shit. I told her you were at the office. Mr. Thomas had us working on a new commercial presentation. I told her we were drinking while working, so you probably passed out. She said that's probably why you weren't answering the office phone. Hurry up and get the fuck home and check on your daughter, man," Josh said in an irritated tone right before he hung up.

Josh and I had been boys since forever, even before we had wives. We both worked at NJ Sports Marketing, handling all types of promotional and marketing needs for different sports, teams, and individual players. Sports was my life. I actually was going to the NFL until I got hurt and wasn't able to play ball anymore. So, I figured I would take a job on dealing with sports.

Once I put my seatbelt on, I peeled off and headed home to check on my favorite girls.

———

I HAD BEEN IN THE HOUSE FOR A COUPLE OF HOURS, AND MY wife, Zyla hasn't said a word to me. Usually, she just goes on with life and doesn't pay the shit I do any mind. I guess me and my bullshit was getting to her. I walked into the kitchen where she was sitting at the table drinking a cup of coffee.

"So, you not gone talk to me at all today?" I asked.

"Who were you with this time?" Zyla asked without even looking up at me.

"Baby, what are you talking about? Josh told me he let you know I was at the office."

"You and Josh are two sorry ass lying muthafuckas. I called Mr. Thomas last night and he told me he didn't have you doing no extra shit at the job. Mark, I'm so over this bullshit! Our daughter was fucking sick and you were laying up with one of your many hoes. Why the fuck am I not enough for you? Why the fuck did we even get married? Do you even love me? I shouldn't have even listened to my mama when she made me marry you because I was pregnant. Shit, stepdaddies seem to be doing a better job these days. Now, who the fuck was you with? It's no need to keep fucking lying. One day you gone come home and me, Zoey, and all our shit gon' be gone," Zyla fussed.

"Zyla, you not taking my daughter nowhere. You can go, but you gone take her to my mama. I keep telling you stop threatening me with taking my daughter away. If you wanna go, you can, but she ain't going a damn place. I was with Kia since you wanna know so bad."

Zyla didn't say shit else. She just got up from the table and walked off with an attitude. Shit, I didn't know what for. She's the one that wanted to know who I was with.

"Daddy!" Zoey screamed and ran right to me.

"Hey, lil' mama. What's up?" I asked, kissing her forehead.

"I'm was sick and mommy took me to the doctor. Him said I fine now. Where you was at, mommy was scared and crying?" Zoey said.

"I was at work, baby, but daddy is here now. You feel better?" I asked.

"Yup...mommy took good care of me."

"Well, since you feel better, how about we go out and get mommy some dinner and gifts? So, we can make her feel better since she always looks out for us. You can't tell her where you going, just tell her you taking a ride with me, okay?"

"Alright, daddy," Zoey said as I put her down. I watched her run off to find her mother. My baby was five now and I don't regret having her straight out of school. Hell, she's the best thing in my life. I fuck up a lot with being a husband, but I'm a damn good daddy.

My phone vibrated in my pocket, alerting me that I had a text message. I pulled the phone out of my pocket and saw it was a message from Kia. She knew not to bother me when I was home. I looked at the text and a smile crept up on my face.

I knew she would see it my way.

K: I decided to get rid of the baby, but I'ma need the money.

Me: I'll bring it to you tomorrow.

K: Ok, I love you.

Me: Don't text me no more while I'm home with my family, Kia. You know better.

I knew after that last text she wasn't gone call me back. I was going to take her this money tomorrow and then I was finished with her. I couldn't deal with chicks anymore once they started to catch feelings.

I hopped in the shower and let the water run over my head. Thoughts of this unhappy marriage I was in, came to mind, and the tears just started flowing down my face. For three years, I have been dealing with Mark's bullshit. At first, I wasn't worried since I was the one with the ring. Now I'm starting to feel like I deserve better than this. Years ago, my parents thought it was a good idea for us to get married since I was pregnant, and Mark was going to the NFL. So, I did what my parent's wishes were. Now don't get me wrong, I loved my husband back then. As a matter of fact, Mark was my first everything. The only man I've ever been with. We started out in high school and been together ever since. At first, I used to think it was me, but shit, I look damn good, and I'm a damn good wife and mother. So, the only thing I could come up with is Mark being a low-down dirty dog.

After I finished washing from head to toe a couple more times, I rinsed then got out of the tub. Mark and Zoey went out for a little while, so I was just going to relax and have me a glass of wine. Once I made it into the bedroom, I sat on the bed to oil my skin. Then I slipped on one of my granny nightgowns from Walmart. Mark hated them, but I didn't give a damn; he wasn't touching me anyway. After

I finished, I made my way into the kitchen to grab me a glass of wine.

As soon as I sat down on the couch, my phone started going off. I was so pissed I left it all the way in the room. I jumped up and ran to grab it in case it was my mama. When I got to the room and saw it was my neighbor, Melissa, from across the street, I was so irked. Her nosey ass didn't want to do shit but talk about people and worry about what was going on around here. Melissa was like the neighborhood watch, but not for safety, just to be fucking nosey. By the time I got the phone, it stopped ringing, but her ass called right back, so I decided to answer. This tea must have been burning a hole in her tongue.

"Yes, Melissa. How can I help you, love?"

"Girl, did you check out the new neighbor that's moving in? Zyla, he is fine as shit with a nice ass car. Come to the door and see him. I didn't see any females or kids. So, you know what that might mean. He's single, girl, and single is right up my alley."

"Melissa, I thought you were married?"

"He married, but I'm not. How many times do I have to tell you this marriage been done for over five years?"

"Well, why he still there?"

"Because his simple ass doesn't wanna leave, so I do me while he here. I keep asking you do you want me to show you my skills. He doesn't wanna go, so we both do what we do. It is what it is."

"Melissa, ya ass is crazy, and I ain't about to be stalking the new neighbor because you think he's fine. Plus, I'm still married."

"I'm sorry to tell you, babes, but you're married, but Mark's not."

"Get ya ass off that dam phone, get over and keep me company!" Melissa's husband was yelling in the background.

"I gotta go. I'll talk to you a little later." I couldn't do shit but shake my head and laugh at her ass. She talks all that shit, but when her husband yells, she jumps. The chick was completely delusional. Hearing about the new neighbor had me wanting to take a peek to see who it was. I hurried and ran in the room and threw on an oversized t-shirt and some tights. Then grabbed my glass of wine and made my way out front to sit on my patio set.

Melissa was right; someone was moving in. There was a big ass moving truck, and two dudes. I knew that one of them had to be the homeowner, because the other man had on the moving company uniform. One of the dudes had on a wife beater showing off all his tattoos. When he turned to look at me, our eyes locked. He was so fucking fine even though he was wearing glasses. I couldn't help but stare at his big arms, light skin, and pretty hair that he had in a bun. I was so into him I didn't even know that Mark and Zoey had pulled up until she came running up on the porch.

"Mommy! Mommy, me and daddy got you something!" Zoey yelled while jumping in my lap in excitement.

"Aww, what did y'all get me, princess?" I asked, kissing my baby on the top of her head.

"You got a nice view?" Mark asked with a mean scowl on his face.

"What are you talking about?" I asked with a raised brow.

"You know what the fuck I'm talking about, so don't play stupid, Zyla."

"Mark, leave me alone. You can stay the fuck out all night whenever you feel like it, but if I look at another nigga, it's an issue. Man, get out my face and go over ya bitch house," I snapped, forgetting all about Zoey sitting in my lap.

"Watch ya mouth around my daughter, Zyla."

"You started and you didn't watch ya mouth around her. Mark, I said what I said now leave me alone," I snapped once more right before heading in the house. When we got in the house, Mark just wouldn't leave the shit alone. I sent Zoey upstairs to play so she wouldn't have to listen to me and her dad arguing.

"Zyla, you better watch how the fuck you talk to me. Your mouth getting real fucking slick," Mark barked, but I didn't pay his dumb ass any mind.

"You better watch how much dick you slanging, because that dick is pretty loose for a married man," I told him sarcastically then walked off. I walked into the living room, looked out the window, and watched as the new fine ass neighbor and the moving guy carried boxes into the house.

"So, you really gonna keep fucking playing me, right?" Mark asked while walking up on me.

"Mark, leave me the fuck alone and go bother your bitch Kia," I told him then walked off. I heard him mumbling, but at that point, I could care less about what the fuck he was talking about.

I heard the door slam, so I figured he must have left, but I didn't give a shit. I was really getting tired of Mark's cheating ass. He just better pray like hell that he don't bring me shit back because I would fuck him up. I walked upstairs to see what Zoey was still up. When I walked into her room, she was playing with her dollhouse. I sat down on the floor next to her and started playing with her.

"Hey, mommy. Do you want to see what me and daddy brought you from the store?" Zoey asked, smiling from ear to ear.

"Sure, baby. What did y'all buy mommy?" I replied. Zyla got up, walked over to her bed and pulled out a bag from her lil' book bag that she carries everywhere. I could tell that it was jewelry from the bag. Zoey handed it to me and when I pulled the box out, it was a beautiful necklace with the matching earrings and bracelet.

"Do you like it, mommy?"

"I love it, princess. It's beautiful," I told her honestly.

"I'm glad you like it. I helped daddy pick it out," Zoey answered cheerfully. I pulled my baby girl down on my lap and placed small kisses on her cheeks. "I love you, baby girl. You want to come help mommy cook?"

"I love you too, mommy. What are we going to cook?"

"Spaghetti," I answered, knowing she would be excited since that was her favorite meal. We walked downstairs and started cooking, but for some reason, all I could think about was my new neighbor. I opened the door to be nosey, but I didn't see him or the moving truck outside. I did see nosey ass Melissa, and I instantly regretted going to the door.

"Girl, did you see that fine ass man that just moved next to you? I'm finna be over here every damn day to get a close up of his sexy ass." I just shook my head at that crazy ass girl because I knew she was serious as hell.

"Girl, Mark might get his shit together once he see that fine ass nigga. I know he got money just by the shit he was moving into the house."

"Melissa, why is your ass so damn nosey? How the hell you know what he was moving into his house from over there," I asked, pointing to her house.

"Okay, so maybe I might have walked by a few times," she said, causing us both to laugh.

"Girl, your ass is crazy, but I gotta go, I need to finish cooking," I told Melissa, closing the door. For some odd reason, I was a little disappointed that my neighbor wasn't outside.

Zoey and I had already eaten dinner without Mark. After dinner, I cleaned up the kitchen then watched Boss Baby with Zoey. When the movie went off, I put Zoey in the bed and tucked her in. This was the second night in a row that Mark hasn't brought his black ass in the house yet and I refused to call him. I was really getting sick of Mark's cheating ways. He hurt me to the core when he told me that he was with some bitch named Kia.

She had to be pretty special for him not to answer any of my calls while I sat in the hospital with our daughter. I was starting to think that Mark and I had outgrown one another. I was starting to threaten him with taking my daughter and leaving more and more. The only thing he would say is I don't care if you want to leave, but you're not taking my daughter anywhere. Mark had to be out of his damn mind if he thought I was gonna leave my daughter behind with his cheating ass. Especially since it was because of his cheating ass ways that I wanted to leave in the first place.

MARK

I had every intention on staying in today to try to make it up to Zyla for being out with Kia while she had to sit in the hospital with Zoey by herself. When I pulled up and caught her eye-fucking the neighbor that was moving in, she made my blood boil. I knew I did me whenever I wanted to, but Zyla had me fucked up if she thought for one moment that she was gonna fuck around on me. And Zyla's smart ass mouth wasn't making that shit any better. As soon as I left out the door, the neighbor was gritting me hard as shit with a smirk on his face. He hadn't even moved in yet and I already didn't like his thug looking ass.

I hopped in my ride and drove straight to Kia's house so I could give her the money for the abortion. I shot Kia a text telling her to open the door because I was on my way. When I walked in the house, I walked straight to the bedroom and found Kia's ass laying on the bed playing with her pussy. All I could do was shake my head. I only planned to drop off the money but the sight of her playing in her pussy caused my dick to brick up immediately. Hell, I was about to hit that. I didn't see the harm in fucking her crazy ass one last time. I stripped out of my clothes and helped her play in her wet pussy until she nutted all over my fingers. I wasted no time sliding in that wet box. She wrapped her legs around my waist, and I beat that pussy up like it was the last time. Kia had some good pussy and I hated to give it up, but her ass was getting too clingy and catching feelings and shit. It was time to cut her loose. After we both nutted, I got up and walked into the bathroom to clean myself up before I put my clothes back on.

"Damn, baby, you leaving me already?" She asked seductively.

"Yes, I'm leaving, Kia. I told you last night that I was only coming to give the money for the abortion, but since you was in here playing with your pussy, I decided fucking you once more wouldn't hurt. Please don't start your shit right now because I'm really not in the mood," I stated.

"Mark, you really think you in control of shit, don't you? You think you can fuck whenever you want and treat women like objects, then go about your business, but you got the wrong bitch when it comes to me. As a matter of fact, give me my fucking money and get the fuck out my house, Mark!" Kia yelled loudly.

"You better watch how the fuck you talk to me, Kia. How much fucking money do you need, and when the fuck is your appointment?"

"It's two grand, and don't worry about when the appointment is, it's not like you're gonna come sit in the clinic with your mistress," Kia barked. I knew I had to get out of there before I smacked that bitch. I know damn well don't no abortion cost that much.

"I didn't say it did, but that's how much it's gonna cost your ass, so either give me the fucking money or prepare to be a fucking daddy plain and simple," she said with her hands on her hip.

"Don't hit my fucking line again," I told Kia before storming out the room.

It had seemed like my life had been spiraling out of control ever since I got hurt.

Mark Holmes drafted to the Philadelphia Eagles straight out of high school.

The thoughts of my past came to mind and always had me fucked up. I didn't even get to play in a real game; my ass got hurt in athletic camp. I was one of the top quarterbacks at Camden High School. I was born in Camden, NJ, but we moved to Cherry Hill, New Jersey my sophomore year of high school. I still stayed At Camden High School to play ball since they had one of the top football teams in New Jersey. You couldn't tell me that I wasn't gonna play in the NFL, but I guess God had other plans being as though I got injured, and those dreams were no longer.

I worked with every sport you can think of, and I loved every bit of my job. Zyla and I met in high school and I fell for her hard. Zyla wasn't like the rest of the hot ass girls that went to our school, and that alone made her special to me. Zyla was a medium brown complexion with a blessed body. She was already thick before she had Zoey, but I swear it seemed like she had gotten even thicker ever since she had my daughter. Zyla was a great woman, which was why I couldn't figure out why the fuck I kept fucking around on her. I talked a lot of shit to Zyla about her leaving if she wanted to, but the truth was, I would lose it and be sick as fuck without her. I swear it felt like I was addicted to fucking other bitches. Maybe I should just see if Zyla was interested in having an open marriage. Maybe that would keep my black ass out the doghouse.

My phone ringing brought me from my thoughts. I looked at the caller id, and it was my boy, Josh. I was sure he was calling to lay my ass out about the shit I pulled last night.

"Hey, Josh. Wassup?" I answered.

"Nigga, I'm surprised your ass allowed to talk on the phone today after that shit you pulled last night. Zyla gonna fuck around and leave your black ass and don't come crying to me about it," he told me.

"Nigga, I don't know why the hell you keep fucking around on Zyla. She's a really good woman, not to mention beautiful. I'm not trying to lecture you, Mark, but you really need to slow down or divorce her."

I sat in front of my house listening to my boy dig in my ass about dogging out my wife. I knew Josh was right about everything that he was saying. I just wish I knew how to stop fucking around on her. Thoughts of Kia being pregnant crossed my mind and I thought about if I should tell Josh or not.

"Yeah, I know, man, I don't even know why I fuck around on Zyla because none of them bitches don't have shit on my wife. But listen, I fucked up badly this time. Kia ass told me she was pregnant. I just gave her ass money to get an abortion," I told him while shaking my head.

"Nigga, you out here raw-dogging these nasty ass bitches, not to mention that you have a fucking wife. Zyla gonna end up killing your ass and she would be in her rights to do so. Mark, you my boy, and I love you to death, but you need to get your shit together," Josh lectured. I couldn't do shit but listen because he was so right.

"Yeah, I know, Josh. Well, I'm in front of the house, so let me get in this house before I get myself in even more trouble," I told him. When we hung up, I got out the car and walked into the house. When I got upstairs, I went into Zoey's room and stared at her sleeping peacefully. I kissed Zoey on the cheek, before leaving out of her room.

When I walked into my bedroom, Zyla was sitting up on the bed going through her phone. She didn't even acknowledge the fact that I was in the room. I stripped out of my clothes and sat on the bed

"Zyla, how long do you plan on not talking to me?" I asked her.

"It depends. How long you plan to fuck around on me."

"Look, I'm sorry that I keep hurting you. Despite what you believe, I hate seeing you hurt. But listen, I was thinking since I seem to have a problem with being faithful, maybe we could have an open marriage. We could both see other people; that way I won't keep hurting you." I looked over at Zyla because she hadn't responded yet and I was trying to figure out if I could tell what she was thinking. Without out saying a word, Zyla charged at me and started hitting me like I was some bitch from the street.

"Have you lost your fucking mind? That's your solution for the problem? You want me to give you permission to fuck other bitches?

And you want me to fuck other men just so you can do what the fuck you want to do? Fuck you, Mark! I hate you!" she yelled. Zyla's voice was laced with so much pain that I instantly felt like shit. I didn't know what else to do. I didn't want to lie and say I'll stop because deep down, I knew I wouldn't. She jumped up, started crying and grabbing shit before darting out the door.

"Zyla where the fuck do you think you're going?"

"Fuck you, Mark! You think you can just fuck around on me then ask me for an open marriage? You are not the man I married and I want out of this marriage!" She yelled while jumping in her car and pulling off. All I could do was shake my head. I knew I couldn't go after her since I had Zoey, and I wasn't about to wake my daughter up to follow behind Zyla. I walked back in the house and peeked into Zoey's room to make sure we didn't wake her up. I hated when we argued when Zoey was around, but sometimes shit happens.

It's been two weeks since my husband asked me for an open marriage, and I was still hurt and felt quite disrespected by his question. I haven't said too much to Mark since that night. He talked to me mainly when Zoey was around because I wanted to be as normal as I possibly could around her. Mark had just took Zoey to Chuck E. Cheese so I could do some housework. My doorbell rang and I wondered who could have been at my door.

"Who is it?" I asked.

"The new neighbor," I heard a man say. When he mentioned who it was, I was eager to see what the hell he wanted. I snatched the door open and we locked eyes just like the first time we saw each other? This was my first time seeing him since the day he moved in.

"Hello...I'm Zyla. Welcome to the neighborhood."

"Hey Zyla, I'm Jaxen, but you can call me Jax. I'm here because I wanted you to know that I was getting some plumbing work done to my house tomorrow morning, and it may interfere with your water. The company said they were going to reach out, but I figured I would still let you know," Jax's fine ass said.

His stare was becoming uncomfortable; it was almost like he could see through my soul. Jax was tall with a husky build. He had the perfect light complexion with tattoos everywhere and even though he wore glasses this man was fine as fuck. Let's not get on his hair and beard he looked as if he had Indian in his family. I also could tell from his jeans; he also had a pretty decent dick print. I knew I had no business looking at this man like this, but hell, I couldn't help myself. At this moment all I was thinking about were them big ass tatted arms wrapped around me.

"Alright, Jax, thanks for coming to tell me. That was extremely nice of you."

"You're welcome, ma. One more thing before I go. You too pretty to be arguing with that clown ass nigga every day. I know it's none of my business, but you too beautiful for all that. He should be in here fucking you crazy all day instead of always arguing with you," Jax said, shocking the fuck out of me. I wanted to be mad at what he said, but I just couldn't. The shit he just spat had me wanting to fuck his ass right here right now.

"You're right; it's none of your business. Thanks again for giving me the heads-up, Jaxen," I said sarcastically right before shutting my door.

I was still kind of shocked, but in the same breath, Jax seemed like that nigga. I could tell a street nigga from anywhere and he was just that. His demeanor had hood written all over it and I didn't want nothing else, but to get to know him. I wasn't sure what it was about him, but shit, I might just take Mark up on his offer of having an open marriage.

As soon as I walked away from the door, there was another knock. I walked back over to the door and pulled it open.

"Who was that hoodlum that was walking away from your door?" My mama asked, being nosey.

"Well, hello to you too, Mama," I said sarcastically.

"I asked you a question, child of mine," my mama said, walking her stuck-up ass straight in my kitchen.

"Mama, that was the new neighbor. He wanted me to know that

he was getting plumbing work done tomorrow, so the water may be off for a little while."

Zina Davis was something else. Her and my father, Brian Davis, had been married for almost thirty years. So, that was the reason why they were so big on marriage. My mama was submissive to her husband, but I couldn't do it and didn't see how she did it for so many years. I guess letting my daddy do whatever he wanted to do to her is what kept their marriage together so long.

"Why did he have to come over here to tell you that? Don't the water company come tell you that?" My mama asked with her lip turned up.

"Mama, I don't know. What brings you here?"

"Mark called your father and of course he sent me to come talk to you. What is wrong with you, girl? That is your husband and the father of your child. I don't know why you insist on pissing that man off."

Mark strikes again. His ass always goes running to my parents, and they always come over here talking to me like whatever he does is fine. I wasn't going to do this with my mama today. I just wish her, and my father would leave me and my marriage the fuck alone.

"Mama, I'm not about to go through this with you today. Did Mark tell y'all that he was laid up with some bitch while I was sitting up in the hospital with Zoey? Did he tell y'all he wants an open marriage? NO! I bet he didn't tell y'all none of that. So, please miss me with the bullshit, mama. I'm not just going to sit around here and let Mark do me dirty. I deserve a man that's going to love me better, and I'm pissed off it took me three years to realize that shit."

"Young lady, you better watch how you talk to me," my mama snapped.

"No, I won't watch how I talk to you. I'm sick of you and daddy being all up in my marriage. If it wasn't for the two of you, I wouldn't be in this situation. But no, I needed to get married because I was pregnant. I wish I didn't pay y'all any mind. Now, if you don't mind, I need to clean my house before my daughter gets home."

My mama didn't say anymore. She just got up and left out of my house with her lip turned up. I didn't give a damn though. It would probably take her months to talk to me again, but I didn't care. I was sick of them being all up in my life. When were they going to realize that I deserved more than a man like Mark in my life?

Two hours went by, and I was finished cleaning the house and cooking dinner. I had made a big pot of Jambalaya so we would have some leftovers for tomorrow in case the water was off long. I was finally sitting down with a glass of wine. Thoughts of Jax came to mind and I wanted to know more about him. The sound of the front door opening brought me out of my thoughts. I thought Zoey was going to come running in, but she was fast asleep in her daddy's arms. I looked at him and turned my attention back to my bottle of wine that was almost gone.

"So, this is what you gone do every day now? Drink a bottle of wine?" Mark asked, coming back into the living room.

"Mark, leave me alone. All you ever do anymore is get on my fucking nerves and stop being a bitch and running to my parents. Nigga, they can't save you no fucking more. As a matter of fact, I think I'ma take you up on your offer. I want an open marriage, so go ahead and stay with one of ya bitches tonight," I said while pouring the last little bit of wine in my glass. The mean scowl on his face showed me that he wasn't feeling what I said, but I didn't understand why. This was his idea.

The thought of Ms. Zyla had been on my mind for a couple of days. I didn't know what it was about shawty, but what I did know is that I wanted her. I normally didn't step on other nigga's toes, but I could tell her husband wasn't worth shit. Her and that pretty little girl deserved better.

"Yo, baby girl next door is fine as fuck. Every time I pull up though she arguing with dude. You know who that is, right?" My right hand Khi asked.

"Yeah, Mark Holmes bitch ass. I peeped that when I first moved in. The nigga that was supposed to get drafted to the Eagles, but he got hurt at football camp."

I been noticed who her husband was, but that didn't stop me from looking at her fine ass on the daily. I actually hated how he treated her. I also hated how they both argued in front of their little girl. The shit wasn't cool at all. I had a daughter of my own and I wouldn't dare do half the shit they do in front of their daughter. She was about the same size as my Jayla, which meant she probably was five or six.

"Jax...you don't hear me talking to you, man?" Khi yelled.

"My fault, man. So what's going on around the way?"

"Nothing different, we still got shit on lock. When you going to meet with the new plug? I hate that B got cased. I hate dealing with new people," Khi stressed.

"Well, I met dude before; it's actually his mans. Just like if something was to happen to me, everyone would be dealing with you. That's just the way business runs, bro."

"Don't get me wrong, I get it, but I just hate dealing with new people. You just can't trust everybody."

"Hell, bro, the life we live, we gotta watch our backs every day. No matter who we deal with."

"I hear you, so how you like living out here?"

"It's quiet and different. I'm really feeling it. I'm still pissed my G-mom wouldn't come with me."

"Now, you know damn well G-mom wasn't coming out here. She set in her ways and you know I got her. I be checking on her all day long. Hell, I get all them good ass meals you be missing."

I had purchased this house for a new start for me and my G-mom. But she wouldn't come with me. She insisted I go alone to start my own life and memories in my new house. I had been in the streets since I was a teenager. Now I had so much money, it was really time for me to start investing so I could start living a better life for me and my daughter. I wanted my G-mom around since she took care of me. I made sure she was good. My mother was killed by her pimp years ago and my pops was somewhere strung out. My G-mom had been taking care of me ever since. She didn't approve of what I did, but as long as I didn't have the drugs in her house, she was cool. She may not have come with me this time, but I was going to keep trying.

"Yeah, I know she set in her ways, but I'ma keep trying to get her down here. Shit, this house big enough for her to have her own space."

"I feel you, man. Shit if you want me to, I'll keep asking too. Did Sasha bring Jayla over here yet?"

"Nah, I haven't given her my address yet. Sasha be on good bullshit, so I'm not even sure if I wanna give her the address. I may just meet her somewhere to get Jayla," I said, causing Khi to laugh.

Sasha and I were once a couple until I broke it off. I had put years into us for her to still be on the same bullshit. I needed someone that was about her shit. I needed someone that was trying to make something out of themselves, especially because of the life that I lived. What if something was to happen to me? What would Sasha have to offer my daughter? Not a damn thing, and that's what I didn't like about her; she had no drive. All she wanted was for me to take care of her. I wanted a Boss chick, a chick that could handle her own.

"Yeah, that's a good idea. Go meet her ass somewhere. If you want, I can pick my goddaughter up and bring her to you whenever you're ready."

Khi was definitely my bro. No matter what me, G-mom, or Jayla needed, he had us and vice versa. We had been friends since we were little. Our parents were close friends until my parents started living a whole different lifestyle.

———

IT WAS THE NEXT DAY AND LOUD BANGING COULD BE HEARD ON my front door. I just knew it was the plumber, but to my surprise, it wasn't.

"So, you got you a new house and wasn't even going to give me the address?"

"Sasha, what are you doing here, and how did you get my address?" I asked while taking a sleeping Jayla out of her arms.

"G-mom told me. You know how she gets when I tell her that Jayla hasn't seen you in a while.

"This bullshit right here is the exact reason why I didn't give it to you. Your ass is always on the bullshit. You know damn well you didn't pop up at my house this early in the morning so my daughter could see me. You just wanted to be on your typical bullshit.

Anyway, now that you have brought her, I'll keep her for a few hours and bring her home later."

"Jax, I'm not leaving my daughter here if I can't come in," Sasha said, rolling her eyes, but I wasn't about to play with her ass.

"Okay, no problem. Here take her back home with you because your messy ass isn't allowed in my house," I told her while passing her my sleeping daughter.

"Really, Jaxen? You're such an asshole; bring my daughter home within two hours," Sasha stated, but I wasn't about to entertain her petty ass.

"Good morning, Jax," Zyla's sexy ass spoke, gaining my full attention. When I looked up, Zyla was wearing a burgundy business pants suit and her hair was in a high ponytail. I was so turned on that I couldn't hide it if I wanted to.

"Hey, Zyla. You look beautiful," I told her.

"Thank you," she replied while walking to her car.

"Really, Jaxen?! You're really flirting with that bitch right in front of me like I'm not fucking standing here?" Sasha snapped. I was so distracted by Zyla that I forgot that Sasha's annoying ass was even on my doorstep.

"First of all, Sasha, what I do or who I flirt with isn't any of your concern. Now you claim you popped up to bring me my daughter, well I have her. So if you don't mind, I need to go. I have shit to do," I told Sasha, closing my door. I hated talking to my daughter's mother like that, but Sasha was a piece of work. She could be annoying as fuck and I wasn't beat for her ass. I made a mental note to call my grandmother and tell her off about giving Sasha my address.

While Jayla was sleep, I decided to make the two of us some breakfast. I made waffles, sausage, and cheese eggs. That was one of my baby girl's favorite meals. I heard a knock on the door, and I was for sure this time that it was the plumber since no one else knew where I lived. I opened the door and let them in. Once we went over what they were gonna do, I walked back into the living room and Jayla was now sitting up on the couch looking around the unfamiliar house. When I stood in front of her, she jumped into my arms and hugged me tightly.

"Daddy, I missed you!" she yelled.

"Hey, daddy's princess. I missed you so much." I hugged her even tighter.

"Where are we? This house is nice."

"This is our new house; you have your own room with lots of surprises waiting for you. I'll take you upstairs and show it to you as soon as we finished eating breakfast." After Jayla and I finished eating breakfast I took her upstairs and showed her the rest of the house, but I saved her room for last. When we walked into her room, Jayla's face lit up like it was Christmas morning.

"Daddy, this is my new room?" Jayla quizzed.

"Yes, princess, this is all yours. whenever you come over, this is your own space," I assured Jayla.

"Yay, I love it!" Jayla said excitedly, jumping up and down.

"I'm glad you like it, baby. Go ahead and play in here for a few. I have to take you back home soon," I told her.

I had her entire room done in unicorn décor since she loved unicorns and her bed frame customized with her name on it; my baby room was fly. She loved it and that's all that mattered to me.

———

JAYLA AND I WERE HAVING SO MUCH FUN TOGETHER THAT I LOST track of time and the entire day seemed to fly by. After the plumber left, Jayla and I headed out as well. I stopped and grabbed some McDonald's on the way to Sasha's house for Jayla. I wasn't a fan of McDonald's, but my baby loved it. I walked Jayla up to the door and knocked. Sasha's best friend, Amanda, opened the door and let me in.

"Hey, Jax," Amanda spoke in a flirty tone. I knew Amanda wanted to fuck since the first day I met her hoe ass, but no matter how much Sasha got on my nerves, I would never do no shit like that. I just nodded my head and waited for Sasha to come downstairs.

"Mommy, look what I got?" Jayla said, showing Sasha her food from McDonald's.

"Jayla, go to the table and eat so I can talk to mommy. I love you, princess," I told Jayla, giving her a kiss on her cheek.

"What do you need to talk to me about, Jax?" Sasha blurted, breaking me from my thoughts.

"I'm gonna be picking Jayla up every other weekend. She has her own room, clothes and sneaks already, so you don't have to send her with anything. I'll pick her up from school on the weekends that I get her."

"Whatever, Jaxen. You just bet not have none of your bitches around my daughter or you'll never see her again," Sasha barked.

"I don't know who the fuck you think you talking to like that, but I'll do what the fuck I want with my daughter. If you ever threaten to keep my daughter away from me again, I promise you it won't be pretty," I warned Sasha's ass then walked out the door.

Sasha had me all the way fucked up telling me what to do with my daughter. Jayla was my everything and I loved her more than life itself. I would kill Sasha if she ever tried to keep my daughter from me. I pulled up to G-mom's house to see what she was up to, and to find out why she gave my crazy ass baby mama my address without asking me first. Before I could knock on the door, my G-mom had already opened it.

"Hey, old lady. Wassup?" I asked, kissing her on the cheek.

"Not a damn thing. How's the new house coming along?" She asked.

"It's great, but it would be better if you moved in with me," I told her.

"Boy, I don't know how many times I have to tell your hard-headed ass that I'm not leaving my house. I'm fine right where I am. Sasha stopped by here this morning, so I gave her the address to where you were."

"Yeah, I know. Why would you give her crazy ass my address? I didn't tell her where I lived for a reason."

"Boy, don't nobody give a damn about your reasons. Sasha is the mother of your child. Y'all negros love to call women crazy once y'all break up. Sasha wasn't crazy when your ass was in the pussy," my G-mom stated seriously. All I could do was shake my head because this old lady had no chill. My G-mom was more hood than me and most of the niggas I know, but on the flip side, she was the sweetest woman I know. I sat and talked with my favorite lady for a little over an hour. After she made me a plate to go, I got in my car and headed home.

The ride to my new home was quiet because I didn't even bother to turn the radio on. I just let my mind run free. Thoughts of Ms. Zyla ran freely in my mind once again and made me want to get to know everything about her. When I saw her this morning wearing that business suit, I just wanted to pull every piece of clothing off her, piece by piece and dive in between her thighs.

When I pulled up to my house, I was praying I would see Zyla, but instead, I saw her punk ass husband walking to his car. It was damn near ten at night, so he must have been on his creep shit. I watched him make a phone call before pulling out the driveway. All I could do was shake my head because that nigga didn't know what he had at home.

As I was walking up to my house, a thought came to mind. I took my food in the house then walked next door. I knew I was probably out of line but I needed to see Zyla. I walked up to the door and lightly tapped on the door. I didn't want to wake her daughter if she was sleeping. When Zyla opened the door, she was wearing a pair of grey tights with a black t-shirt.

"Jaxen, what are you doing here?" She asked in a surprise tone.

"I came over here since I saw that clown ass nigga leave. I know I'm overstepping my boundaries, but I don't give a fuck. I'm the type of nigga that goes after what he wants. So, what you up to tonight, Ms. Zyla?" I asked with a smirk on my face.

"Well, since you know you're overstepping your boundaries. Why the fuck are you still standing here?" Zyla asked with her lip turned up, about to slam the door in my face. I put my foot in the doorway to keep her from slamming it on me.

"Come on, little mama, be nice. Slamming the door in my face would have been so rude," I said with a big smile on my face.

"Jax, what makes you think I would even be interested in a man that wants me but he knows I'm married?"

"First off, beautiful, this marriage is over. I could tell by the way you two interact. Secondly, I know for sure I could take you from that clown. All I need is one date and I'm sure we will become the best of friends. Just let me treat you the way you supposed to be treated for one whole night. If you don't like it, I'll move on, but if you do like it, I'll be ready for the next date."

"Alright, Jax. Give me your phone. I'll put my number in, but only on one condition."

"What might that be, beautiful?" I asked with a raised brow.

"You don't show up here at my house. Now, is that a deal?" I nodded my head and handed her my phone. Now that I knew I had her where I wanted her, I didn't need to show up at her house. I had a home of my own that I was sure she would be in sooner than later.

MARK

"**D**amn baby girl, you smell good as fuck." I beamed as I nuzzled my nose in Kia's neck. When Zyla started talking that shit about an open relationship, I walked right out the door on her. I knew what the fuck I had said, but I didn't mean that she did the shit too. I wish her ass would let me catch her with anybody. Besides, she always had Zoey, so I knew that wasn't going down.

"Thank you, Mark. Now, can we go into the bedroom or are you going to fuck me right here in the living room?" Kia cooed, licking her lips.

I chuckled at her little ass while pinning her up on the wall. "You already know it don't matter to me. We can do that shit in here, in there, or out front. I don't give a damn as long as we just straight fucking, no talking. Are you sure you good to do this? I know it's only been two weeks since the abortion," I inquired.

"I'm good, baby. I'm not in no kind of pain. If anything, I'm excited to know that I got you for the whole night. Plus, the bleeding stopped the other day." Kia and I may argue, but we always manage to find our way back to each other. I had been missing her like crazy. Well, missing her pussy like crazy. Zyla was on good bullshit and wouldn't even let me touch her. Every now in then she would at least let me hit so she could get her own rocks off, but not lately. My wife wouldn't even kiss my black ass. It was something going on with her, and I was soon going to address it.

As soon as I pinned Kia up on the wall, I lifted her up, and she wrapped her legs around my waist. Kia's pretty ass stared at me and watched my every move while I started to kiss her hungrily. While I was kissing her, I slipped my free hand up under her shirt and started to play with her nipples. Kia let out a soft moan letting me know she was enjoying the feeling. While still holding her up on my waist, I walked her to the back of the house where her bedroom was. When we made it to the bedroom, I laid her on the bed on her back. She gave me an intense stare while I stripped out of my clothes. I then watched Kia come out of her clothes.

Once we both were completely naked, I climbed on top of her, and started kissing on her neck. The way she smelled today was definitely doing something to me. I didn't know if it was a new scent or if it was because of how much I was missing her crazy ass. I then moved down to her breasts making sure to show them both some love. My mans was now brick hard and tired of all the foreplay. I wanted to dive straight in Kia's wetness. Once I eased inside of her, I was in heaven; the shit felt so fucking good. She was so wet, just the way I liked it. I stop for a minute to try to get my shit together because the last thing I wanted was to cumm all fast.

"Fuck, ma! This shit right here feels so good. This dick been missing you, girl." I beamed right before I started stroking Kia's fine ass nice and slow. She was fucking me from the bottom, meeting me stroke for stroke. It was like our bodies were intertwined. This here wasn't no straight fucking shit; it was like we were making love.

I leaned down in her ear and whispered, "You miss this dick, don't you?" It was like the more I talked to her, the wetter her pussy got. I then started speeding up the pace giving her faster strokes while I continued to talk my shit.

"Mmm...hmm! Mark, just like that, baby! Just like that! Fuck me, baby!" Kia yelled out in pleasure.

"I'm about to cumm, ma. How about we do this shit together?" I asked, digging all in Kia's guts.

"Whewwww! Mark, I'm cummin', baby! I'm cummin'!" As soon as she screamed out, we both came long and hard, causing both our bodies to be tired and drained. After we both got done breathing all heavy, we looked each other in the eyes and smiled.

"You ready to go get in the shower?" I asked Kia.

"Yes, baby. Come on," Kia said, getting up and leading the way. All I needed now was a nice shower then I would take my ass straight to sleep.

———

THE SMELL OF BREAKFAST COOKING RIGHT ALONG WITH THE SUN shining through the window woke me up. I knew Kia wasn't still lying right next to me because of the smell of cinnamon. Baby girl must have been making her famous banana nut French toast that I loved so much. I put this good dick on her last night, and now she being Betty Crocker and shit. I climbed out of bed, slipped my pants on, and made my way into the bathroom to take a piss and brush my teeth. After I was finished, I walked back into the room and checked my phone. I didn't have any miss calls or text messages from Zyla. I only had messages from my boss. Today was Sunday and I wasn't thinking shit about work. I just wanted to enjoy this day, so I closed out my messages and threw the phone back on the floor next to the bed. Then I headed down to the kitchen to see if Kia was almost finished this food.

Once I made it to the kitchen, Kia was standing at the stove shaking all that ass with a t-shirt and panties on. I stood back and stared at her for a minute wondering where the music was coming from until I noticed she had the Air Pods in her ears. Kia still hadn't noticed me staring at her, so I decided to walk up behind her. The minute I grabbed her around her waist, she turned around and slapped the shit out of me.

"Fuck, girl! Why you hit me like that?" I yelled, grabbing the side of my face.

"Shit! Baby, I'm sorry. I didn't even know you were in here. Why would you grab me knowing I couldn't hear shit?" Kia said, running over to me.

"My fault. I was just trying to surprise you, but anyway, what you in here cooking up?"

"I made you some banana French toast, turkey bacon, cheese eggs, and some fresh-squeezed orange juice. Sit down while I fix your plate. I was just about to come get you because I was finished cooking," Kia replied, walking over to the stove to fix my plate.

I sat down at the table and watched her while she maneuvered around getting my food together. Kia could be a pain in the ass, but other times she was cool peoples. I think I got used to being around her when Zyla was tripping, and then when Kia was tripping, I would take my black ass home. *I guess my selfish ass just wanted them both*, I shook my head at my own thoughts.

"Here you go, baby," Kia said, placing my plate in front of me and leaning down to kiss my cheek.

"Thanks, ma! So, what you doing today?" I asked.

"Nothing, just was chilling in the house today since it's Sunday and I don't have to work. What you got planned?" Kia asked while walking back over to the table with her plate.

"I was hoping I could chill with you today. You don't have any company coming over, do you?"

"No. I keep telling you I don't deal with anyone like that but you, Mark. I don't know why that is hard for you to believe me. I know you're married, but that doesn't mean I have to deal with other people because you deal with someone. It's been a minute since I've been checking for anyone else. It's been only you for a minute now. What do I have to do to make you believe that it'll always be Team Mark?" Kia asked with sad eyes.

"No need for the sad face, ma. I'm just shocked, that's all. I never not one time expected you not to deal with anyone else. That would be selfish of me to ask you to do that and I'm still with my wife."

"Mark, I already told you I'm fine with what we are as long as I get some of your time too. Who knows, later on I may wanna see someone else, but I'm fine right now just being all yours. Now, let's finish eating so we could lay up and cuddle."

Once we finished our food, we made our way back to the bedroom where we laid up, fucked and fucked some more 'til we drifted back off to sleep.

I was so happy today because I received my acceptance letter to get into business school. I had been putting my future on hold because of this marriage and being a mother. I regretted being a stay at home mom. I sat back and thought about everything I put on hold to make this marriage work, listening to my parents, and I'm so fucking mad. Long talks with Melissa and Jax had me thinking about me and Zoey's future. I had to come to terms with Mark and I not being together in the future, so I had to be able to take care of my baby alone.

I wasn't mad about that because I was kind of over my husband these days. His ass had really been staying out a couple nights a week then rolling up in here like we were still a happily married couple. My ass had started sleeping in our guest room. I wasn't fucking with Mark's dirty dick ass, and he hated it. But he made his own bed now his selfish ass could lay in it. My phone went off alerting me that I had a text message.

Jax: What you doing, beautiful?

Me: Trying to figure out how I'm going to celebrate tonight. I received my acceptance letter.

Jax: That's what's up, ma! I'm proud of you.

Me: Thank you so much, Jax. I really appreciate you.

Jax: How about you let me take you out to eat or something? Or is baby girl there?

Me: No, she's not here. My parents are keeping her for the night and taking her to school in the morning. They said they'll give me a break, which shocked the hell out of me.

Jax: Well, since you're free. Are we going to eat or what?

Me: Yes, we can go eat. Give me an hour and I'll be ready.

Jax: Ok. See you shortly, beautiful.

It was something about the way he said beautiful that made me all warm and tingly inside. I had already chilled with Jax a couple of times and I was really feeling his company. He was such a gentleman and I was enjoying him. I hurriedly got up from my couch then headed into my bedroom to find something to wear. The weather was slightly changing and it was the time of the year where you didn't need a coat, but you still needed a small jacket. I settled on a pair of ripped jeans and off the shoulder hunter green sweatshirt. I probably won't be wearing a jacket, but I put on my hunter green Ugg's. I was not really feeling like bothering with this hair of mine, so I was going to put it up in a high ponytail.

Once I decided on what I was wearing, I made my way into the bathroom so I could shower. I locked the bathroom door in case of Mark coming in. The last thing I needed was his ugly ass trying to get into the bathroom with me. I turned the water to the temperature I like then jumped in. I enjoyed the warm water running down my body so much I almost wanted to stay in there, but I knew I was on a time frame. After washing and rinsing a couple of times, I hopped out the shower and started to dry my body off. I slipped on my silk robe and made my way into my bedroom to oil my skin then slip my clothes on. A couple of minutes later, I was already to go. I shot Jaxen a text letting him know that I was heading out the door. I got in my car, pulled around into Jaxen's garage and hopped in the car with him. It was my idea to go around to his garage. The last thing I wanted was Mark to see me getting in the car with the neighbor.

"Damn, you smelling good enough to eat," Jaxen said as he climbed into the car.

"Thanks," I replied with a flirty smile. I couldn't lie; Jaxen was a really cool dude and kept me laughing, which was more than what my sorry ass husband was doing. Mark was making it easier and easier for me to hang out with Jaxen.

"What do you have a taste for?"

"Let's go to Carrabba's," I answered. On the way to the restaurant, I called Zoey to check up on her before she went to bed.

Twenty minutes later we pulled in the parking lot of Carrabba's and after parking, Jaxen walked around to open my door. Before we walked into the restaurant, I powered my phone off giving Jaxen the same respect that he gives me when we go out. He didn't take calls while we were out chilling.

Once we were seated, I decided to order a Henny punch. I wasn't quite sure what that was, but it sounded good. I wasn't much of a drinker, but I was there to celebrate. We placed our order and waited for our drinks. I then showed Jax my letter and watched him smile as he read it. Jax wore a proud look on his face and that made me think of Mark. I should have been celebrating with my husband instead of Jaxen, but I'm almost sure he was laid up with the next bitch. I more than likely wouldn't see his black ass until the morning sometime.

"I'm really proud of you, Zyla. Just know that this is just the beginning of our celebration," Jaxen's, sexy ass, stated.

"Thanks, Jax," I replied. The waiter brought our food out and we both quickly dove in. We stayed and talked for about an hour after we were done eating. We covered everything from how Jaxen first got involved in the street shit, down to his baby mother Sasha and his daughter Jayla. For the first time since we've been hanging out, I told him about the history of me and Mark.

Finally, we pulled in Jaxen's garage so I could retrieve my car. Jaxen opened the door for me and that's when I realized that I was tipsier than I thought I was.

"I'm not letting you drive, so I'll drive you to the front or you can walk to the house and get your car tomorrow," Jaxen stated.

"I'm fine to drive, but you can drive my car to the front if that makes you feel better," I told him. There was an awkward silence between the two of us and I couldn't help. I leaned over and kissed Jaxen's lips and he welcomed my tongue into his mouth. Jaxen was the only other man that I've kissed besides Mark, and Jaxen had Mark beat in the kissing department. Jaxen broke the kiss, but I didn't want it to stop.

"Come on because if you keep kissing me like that, I'm gonna take you in my house and fuck the shit out of you," Jaxen boldly stated. I knew I wasn't ready for that, so I walked to my car and got in. Although I wasn't ready to cross that line with Jaxen, my pussy was telling me to let him fuck me, but I refused to listen to that bitch; she was just horny. When we pulled around to the front, I was shocked as hell to see Mark's car parked in the driveway, but I didn't even care.

Jaxen passed me my keys and waited for me to go in the house before he went in. When I walked in the house, all the lights were on. I guess he heard me come in because before I could make it to the bedroom, he was staring me in my face giving me the look of death.

"Zyla, where the fuck you been at all damn night long and where the fuck is my daughter?!" Mark yelled. I didn't know if it was the liquor or the tone in my husband's voice, but I found Mark's questions funny. I laughed in Mark's face then walked in the bedroom. Of course, Mark followed behind me still talking shit. I really wished he would have stayed his black ass out another night instead of fucking with me.

"Mark, Zoey is fine. She's with my parents, but as far as where I was, that's none of your concern. I don't question you about your whereabouts, so don't question me about mine. If I would have known your ass was coming in tonight, I would have stayed out. Now, if you don't mind, I'm going to bed," I told Mark. Then I stripped out of my clothes and climbed into bed, leaving Mark standing there looking mad and stupid.

MARK

Zyla had me all the way fucked up, coming in the house after midnight without my daughter. I swear Zyla was gonna make me fuck her ass up if she kept playing with me. As long as me and Zyla have been together, she has never come in that late, let alone turned her phone off. When she came in popping off at the mouth, I wanted to punch her in her face. I knew Zyla was only mad because I had been staying out more. I couldn't deny that I've been spending more time with Kia ever since she got the abortion.

Kia was just easier to deal with, especially with the way shit was with me and my wife. I still loved Zyla with everything in me, but shit just wasn't the same with us. I knew I was the reason why they weren't, but I wanted what I wanted, and she wasn't willing to give it to me. I was being selfish, but that's' just how it was. I knew that Zyla wouldn't leave me because she loved my black ass too much. After Zyla got in the bed, I was so pissed with her ass that I decided to sleep in the living room.

The next morning I was woken up from the sound of music playing from the bedroom. I walked in the room and Zyla was dancing in the mirror as she fixed her hair. Zyla was fully dressed and it wasn't even ten in the morning yet.

"Where you headed to?" I asked Zyla, but she didn't even bother to look at me. When Zyla was finished doing her hair, she finally turned around to face me.

"Since my daughter isn't here, I'm going out for the day if you must know," Zyla answered calmly. I wasn't sure what the hell had gotten into my wife, but I wasn't feeling it. Without saying another word, Zyla brushed past me and headed out the door.

I didn't have time to argue with her, so I just let her go. Besides, I had to be at the office in an hour, so I needed to get ready. After showering and getting dressed, I headed out the door, and the neighbor that I didn't like was standing outside like it was summertime. That nigga really rubbed me the wrong way with that smug look on his face. I always catch him checking out my wife. Hell, I be swearing she be checking out his hoodlum looking ass too. They both better tread lightly. The way my mind is set up, I would kill both of their asses if they ever crossed the line. I mean-mugged the fuck out of him before getting in my car.

———

The workday was finally over. I had been calling and texting Zyla's ass all day long, but she refused to answer the phone, so I decided to go have a drink with Josh. After work, Josh and I met at the bar around the corner from the job.

"Wassup, Mark? You don't seem like yourself right now. Is everything good?"

"Yeah, I'm good, but shit with me and Zyla is crazy right now. We ain't fucking, and last night when I got home, Zyla or Zoey both weren't home. I called her ass for hours and she didn't answer. She didn't get her ass in the house until after midnight. And when I asked her where she was, she had the nerve to tell me not to question her. When I got up this morning, she was fully dressed, but she wouldn't tell me where she was going."

"Was she okay because that's like not Zyla to keep Zoey out that late?" Josh stated.

"That's the other crazy thing, Zoey was with Zyla's parents, and that shit has never happened before," I told Josh.

"Damn Mark, it sounds like Zyla's pulling a you on you. Now, maybe you'll understand what you put her through. Josh was my boy, but he surely knew how to add salt to the womb. Maybe Zyla decided to take you up on your open marriage proposal," Josh stated, pissing me off even more.

"Yo', man, why the hell do you always do that shit? I don't always want to hear that shit. Sometimes, I just need you to listen."

"My bad, Mark. I guess I can get carried away sometimes. I just be trying to help you and keep it one hundred with you because you be tripping sometimes," Josh replied.

While I was at the bar, Kia was steady blowing up my phone like she was my damn woman. Her ass was seconds from getting cursed out. She knew better than to call me while I was out.

Kia: Baby, I miss you. Are you coming through tonight?

Kia: You don't have to ignore me, I guess your precious little wife must be around.

Me: Kia, you must've lost your fucking mind, blowing up my phone and texting me this bullshit. I told you not to fucking contact me when I'm not there. If I'm coming through, I'll let you know. Kia, don't do that shit again, and to answer your question, nah, I'm staying home tonight. Don't fucking text my phone again tonight.

Kia: Fuck you, Mark. I'm sick of you treating me like I'm just a side chick.

After reading Kia's last message, I had to do a second look at my phone because I must have read it wrong. I wasn't sure who the fuck Kia thought she was to me, but my side chick was exactly who she was. I knew I shouldn't have started fucking with her ass after she got the abortion. Before putting my phone away, I decided to text my wife to see what she was up too.

Me: Hey, babe. Are you home? I was thinking maybe we could go grab dinner tonight. Shit is getting crazy with us and I just want to talk.

Me: Zyla, I know I've been fucking up, but I'm still your husband, and this shit is getting out of hand.

Zyla really wasn't fucking with me and I wasn't feeling that shit. Before I went home, I stopped pass Zyla's parent's house, so I could get my daughter. I missed my Zoey like crazy. My daughter meant the world to me, which was one of the reasons I needed to get my shit together. I knocked on my in-law's doors, and my father in-law answered the door.

"Wassup, young blood? What are you doing here?" My father in-law asked.

"Wassup, pops? I came by to see my baby. I'm not used to her not being home."

"Your daughter is just fine. I would have thought that you would've taken this time to make things right with your wife. From what I'm hearing, you're fucking up pretty bad. I'm not about to lecture you, Mark, but when I gave my daughter away to you, I expected you to love and cherish my daughter.

I'm gonna leave you with this, then I'm gonna let it go. I'm only telling you this because I like you. You better get your shit together before you lose Zyla. She's nothing like my wife. She will leave your ass and act like you never existed. She might put up with your shit for a little bit, but trust me she will leave you," my father in law, Brian, stated. I didn't say anything because I didn't know what to say.

"Daddy!" Zoey yelled excitedly, jumping in my arms.

"Hey, daddy's princess." I kissed Zoey on the cheek.

"Daddy, Nana and Pop-pop said I was staying another night with them. I don't want to go home," Zoey told me.

"I'm not here to pick you up, I missed you and wanted to see you before I went home," I assured Zoey.

"I love you, daddy," Zoey stated, hugging me tighter.

"I love you too, princess. Daddy about to go home. I'll see you tomorrow." I placed Zoey back on her feet and she ran off upstairs. I didn't see my mother in-law, so I figured she wasn't home, and I didn't bother to ask.

When I pulled up to the house once again, Zyla wasn't home for the second night in a row. I just shook my head and walked into the house. The house looked exactly like it did when I left, letting me know that Zyla hadn't been home since she left this morning.

I had been home for a little over an hour and Zyla still wasn't home. Her ass was really tripping. I decided to order me something but realized that I left my phone in the car. When I walked outside, Zyla was just about to walk in the house. She had a huge smile on her face, and I don't know why it angered me so much.

"Zyla, where the fuck have you been? I've been calling and texting you back to back and you have yet to respond. Then you gone walk in here all smiles. What the fuck is really going on, Zyla, and why is my daughter at your parent's house again?" I barked.

"Here you go with the twenty-one fucking questions. I told you yesterday don't question me about my whereabouts. You be doing ya thing, so let me do mine, damn," I snapped.

"I don't know what the hell you got going on, but you're a mother. Not to mention you're a married woman too. Staying out late, coming in here smelling like liquor and dropping our daughter off to a sitter while you do you, is not shit married women do."

"Nigga, please. Don't come out here talking to me all crazy reminding me that I'm a married woman. When you out here fucking like your ass a single man. Do you worry about our vows when you deep stroking the next bitch? Do you remember you're a father when you eating the next bitch pussy?" Zyla yelled, causing the neighbors to come to the front door. Saying that I was embarrassed was an understatement. I couldn't even respond to what she just said. I just continued towards my car to retrieve my phone.

"See, you can't even look me in my face and answer the question. Well, let me answer it for you, NO…that's the fucking answer. Now, Mark, leave me the hell alone. I'm giving you what you asked for. An open marriage so when I'm doing me leave me alone, like I left you alone," Zyla snapped and walked right into the house.

"Ain't no show going on out here. Y'all can take y'all nosey asses in the house!" I yelled at my nosey ass neighbors, Melissa being one of them. I then looked right next store and Thug life was standing on the step still wearing that smug look on his face. I was about to say something then I decided against it. I just grabbed my phone, locked my car up then took my ass in the house.

Shit with Zyla and I started getting heated. All this kissing and grinding shit like we were horny teenagers was getting on my nerves, but I respected the fact that she is still married. Even though I know her husband ain't worth shit. It had been a couple weeks and we had been kicking it hard going out on dates and all that good shit. Today I wanted to take her shopping, but she wasn't feeling that idea. Although her and Mark were playing a dangerous game with this open marriage shit, I was kind of enjoying spending time with her. I just knew I couldn't put my all into it because she belonged to someone else.

"So, what brings you out tonight? Last I checked you been hanging tough with the neighbor," Khi asked.

"Yeah I know but I feel like I need to step back a little. She wanna be all lovey dovey kissing me and shit. I'm not trying to go there with her if she ain't ready. I mean, I don't give a fuck about her husband, but I ain't trying to put my feelings out there like that."

"Oh, you're feeling her, huh?" Khi asked.

"I hate to admit it, but yeah. I have to respect the fact that she's married though."

"Well, I thought they had an open marriage going on?"

"They do, but I ain't trying to be nobody's long term side nigga. That's why I haven't took it there with her. I'm not trying to confuse her. I mean, I don't think she loves her husband anymore, but these days you can't be too sure. These chicks be in love with these no-good ass niggas all the time."

"I see what you mean. You wanna see how she really feel before you take shit to the next level. Right now, the dating stage is something light, but once sex gets involved, things get hectic."

"Exactly my point. Enough about that shit, let's get some strippers, drinks and food over here. I need to find me a candidate for tonight. A nigga needs some pussy in the worse way, and I'm not trying to go there with Sasha. Then again, I may swing over there and stay the night with her and my daughter." Khi looked at me and shook his head, while he signaled a couple of the strippers over to us. One was light and one was dark. I pulled the dark one in my lap and pulled some money out my pocket.

"I want you to dance on me until I tell you to go, and don't worry I'll make sure you're paid well," I whispered in her ear right before bringing my attention back to Khi.

"All this ass around here... you sure you wanna go there? Sasha ass crazy as fuck, and you know it. You gone fuck around and spend the night with her and she gone think y'all back together again."

"You know I don't be doing all that crazy shit no more. A stripper can give me a lap dance or suck my dick and get me ready for what I got at home. Nothing more, nothing less. Besides, Sasha knows what it is," I assured Khi.

"Well, if y'all got that understanding, then do you. Just be careful, man because Sasha is definitely an unstable creature. I told you that before you even started messing with her, but you just wouldn't leave her nut ass alone."

Khi was right, but it was something about Sasha that had me drawn in when I first met her. Then the sex started and ya boy was gone. It took me years to realize that Sasha was selfish and only gave a damn about herself. Once I realized that she wasn't someone I wanted to spend the rest of my life with, I ended the relationship. The minute I did that, she found out she was pregnant, so I decided to stay to try and give my princess a two-parent home. Of course, that shit didn't work, so now we co-parent. We dibble and dabble every now and then with no strings attached, so I knew she would be fine with me coming over. I shot her a text to let her know that her house would be my last stop for the night.

Me: Hey, ma. You up?

BM: Yes, Jax…what do you want?

Me: I'm coming over to spend the night with you and Jayla.

BM: You not coming to spend the night with Jayla, Jax. You coming to get some pussy, we been past the lying stages. The key is under the mat.

Me: See you a little later.

Khi was right; Sasha was crazy as fuck. All she had to do was say ok, but she had to be a smart ass. I couldn't do shit but shake my head at her craziness. I looked up and light skin was up on Khi while he was smoking. I noticed they had put a bottle and some glasses right next to me. I was all in my phone texting Sasha while the stripper was doing her thing. I didn't even notice the waitress came over here. I poured me a glass and threw that thing back, while I gazed at baby girl that was dancing on me.

———

I GROANED OUT IN PLEASURE WHILE SASHA GYRATED ON MY dick. I had come in from the strip club feeling nice and horny as fuck. When I walked in her room, I could tell through the thin sheet that she was ass naked and ready for the kid. I flipped her little ass over and laid her on her back. I wasn't ready to bust a nut just yet. I was enjoying the feeling of her tight, gushy walls. Due to work and fooling around with Zyla, I hadn't been fucking nobody.

I lifted her legs and threw them on my shoulders while I pumped in and out of her rough as fuck, not showing her no mercy. Sasha loved the rough shit. I wasn't off that shit all the time, but tonight, I didn't mind because that was when Sasha got real nasty with it.

"Fuck Jax! Go harder, baby! Go harder," Sasha moaned out in pleasure.

Sasha had some good pussy to match her crazy ways. I once loved the shit out of this girl, but I just couldn't get past her craziness. She would say time and time again that she wanted us to be a couple, but she just wouldn't act right. I felt myself about to cum, but I wasn't going out like that. I needed her to get her shit before I got mine, so I pulled out and went down. I decided to give her some of this tongue game.

"Oh my God! Jax, this shit feels so good," Sasha moaned.

After I sucked, licked, and slurped on her clit, I felt her body starting to shake, so I hurried and eased right back in her tunnel. The wetness and the warmth put together while she tightened her muscles on my dick was it for me.

"Fuck, Sasha! I'm about to cumm, sweetheart! How about we make this happen together?" I grunted as we both came good and hard together. Thank God I had a condom on. I was sure it would have been another Jayla in the oven if we didn't use protection.

"Damn, boy that shit was everything. You been missing this pussy, huh?" Sasha asked.

"Sasha, take ya ass to sleep, ma," I chuckled.

I didn't come here to pillow talk. I came here to get my dick wet and to get some sleep then I was going to get up and take my baby girl to breakfast.

"You always take shit so serious. You come here and fuck my brains out then all I'm supposed to do is go to sleep. Jax, I don't like what we are becoming," Sasha sassed.

I didn't feel like doing this with her, so I hopped up and made my way to the bathroom to get cleaned up. I thought I was going to spend the night, but nope, I was going to just take my ass home. When I got finished in the bathroom, Sasha was standing outside the door.

"Sasha, why are you standing here looking all crazy?" I asked in annoyance.

"I don't want you to leave, Jax. I'm sorry. I'll just lay back down and go to sleep. I just hate that you're so short with me lately. I know we not together, and that's how it's going to be, but I would still like it if we had some type of friendship."

The sad look in her eyes kind of had me fucked up. I guess I was being a little mean, but as long as she understood that we weren't going to be together, it couldn't hurt us being friends. I grabbed her by her hand, and we both walked back over to the bed. I kissed her lips, pushed her back on the bed and then climbed back on top of her. Sasha and I ended the night with another round before we drifted off to sleep.

Mark had been doing different shit for the past couple of weeks. He had been home chilling and I had been out with Jax. The crazy part was he even had Zoey home with him. This was not my husband, so I was starting to get a little confused. I decided to cook us dinner so we could talk so I dropped Zoey off at my parents. I wanted the house to be empty in case we got into an argument like always.

It was almost time for Mark to get home, so I hurried to set the table. I had cooked chicken parm, garlic knots, and a caesar salad. The sound of the front door opening bought me out of my thoughts. I didn't go see who it was because I knew it was Mark. I just continued to finish getting the table together.

"Hey, baby. It smells good in here, what you cooking?" Mark asked while walking into the kitchen.

"Things have been a little strange between us, so I figured I would cook us a nice dinner. We really need to talk about what we got going on, Mark. I'm a little confused because you say one thing then you do another. So, I'm ready for us to discuss this. Dinner is ready, but you can go ahead and shower and when you finish, we can eat," I said. Mark gave me a head nod and walked off. The minute he walked away; I heard my phone vibrating on the counter. I picked it up and saw I had a text message from Jax.

Jax: I see you not talking to a nigga no more.

Me: I've just been busy, Jax.

Jax: You don't have to lie to me, ma. If y'all trying to make it work, I'll stop texting you.

Me: Can I text you later when I'm finished cleaning the kitchen?

Jax: You can do whatever you want, beautiful. This ya world.

I didn't even respond to him because truthfully, I didn't know what was going on. I was starting to feel him and had I started kissing on him and shit. I had to step back a little before some shit I didn't want to happen, happened. Don't get me wrong, I liked Jax a lot and enjoyed chilling with him, but when I noticed my husband doing shit the right way, I kind of got confused. That's why we needed to have this talk. When I heard Mark coming down the steps, I slid my phone in my pocket and placed his plate on the table. Once he was seated, I got my plate and drink then I sat across from him. He sat there and stared at me for a second before he started eating.

"Is there something wrong?" I asked.

"No...I was just acknowledging how beautiful my wife is." I smiled at him before cutting into my food. Nothing was heard throughout the kitchen but us eating, so I decided I would start the conversation off.

"What is going on between us, Mark?" I asked.

"I know I hurt you time and time again. I know I said I wanted us to have an open relationship, but I'm not sure if that's something I can deal with. Seeing you change has me scared and I opened my eyes to a lot of shit. The last thing I want is another man to come in and take my beautiful wife away from me."

"What makes you think it's another man involved, Mark? I never bought no one home. I never stayed out all night. Tell me what makes you so sure I was seeing another man."

"Because I know my wife. You changed your perfume, your panties and bras got sexier, and you started talking to me like I was the next nigga. That wasn't nothing but another man giving my wife attention, and I don't like that shit one bit. So, I figured it was time for me to get my shit together and sit my ass down. I love you with all my heart, Zyla, which is why I don't want our marriage to end. If you want, we can do counseling to get this shit straight," Mark expressed seriously.

"Why did you say you wanted an open marriage if that's not what you wanted? I would have never thought about going out of my marriage for anything. What's wrong with me, Mark? Am I not enough for you that you need to go elsewhere to get it?"

"Zyla, you're good, baby. I swear you good in every way. You're all the woman I need. I was just on some dumb shit and trust me I've learned my lesson the minute I saw you about to give all my goods to someone else."

Hearing Mark say all of that had me in a better mood. I was starting to feel like we would never get right, but to hear him say he will get counseling was music to my ears. I promised my parents I would try counseling before I threw my whole marriage away. So, I guess this was our first step to trying to get it back on the right path. Mark and I finished our dinner over laughs and enjoyed each other's time. It was a great feeling after dealing with all the bullshit we had been dealing with.

———

I WAS WASHING DISHES WHEN I FELT MARK WRAP HIS ARMS around my waist. Being in his arms felt like old times, and I was loving every bit of it. I shut the water off, dried my hands then turned to face my husband. I pulled him in, stood up on my tippy toes and kissed his lips hungrily. It had been a minute, and I needed and wanted my husband. Mark lifted me up and I wrapped my legs around his waist. Mark then walked me over to the dining room table and sat me on it. Mark gave me a smirk right before he started pulling at the tights I had on. Once he got them off, he placed one of the dining room chairs in front of me, opened my legs, and made contact with my pussy, while licking his lips. I haven't had this type of attention from my husband in a long time.

"Mmm...I miss this shit so much, baby. I can't wait to make you feel good. So, you sit right there and enjoy the ride," Mark beamed before placing his lips on my precious jewel. The minute he began to lick, suck, slurp, and kiss all over my kitty, I was in heaven. Mark had been the only man I've been with, so it wasn't nothing for my body to react to his every touch. I had my eyes closed, enjoying the feeling he was continuing to give my body.

"Dammit, Mark, do it just like that. I've missed you so much, baby," I moaned.

"I've missed your sexy ass, too." Mark managed to get out between licks and sucks.

He continued to move his tongue on my clit rapidly while sliding two of his fingers inside of my opening. The friction from his tongue and the motion from his fingers going in and out of me, caused me to scream out in pleasure.

"Come on, baby. I wanna finish this in the bedroom," Mark said, picking me back up and I wrapped my legs around his waist tight. We enjoyed a passionate kiss on our way to the bedroom. Once we made it to the room, Mark dropped me on the bed and stared at me while he undressed. Watching him like a hawk, I took the rest of my clothes off too.

"I missed this attention, Mark, and I hope we can continue to be happy after the talk we had today."

"We good, baby. I promise you that. Now, let me make love to you like I used to," Mark said, climbing on top of me. Nothing else was heard throughout the room, but soft moans as my husband and I explored each other's body for the rest of the evening.

I was at home blasting music while I cooked dinner, Jaxen was on his way over here and I knew he would be hungry. Jax and I have been kicking it hot and heavy. It was about time that nigga came to his senses when it came to me. Jaxen will always belong to me. I heard the door open and I knew it was him and Jayla. Jax took Jayla to get some clothes and a bunch of other shit I'm sure she didn't need.

"Mommy, look what daddy brought me," Jayla said, holding up her bags. Jax was forever spoiling that little girl. After Jayla finished showing me all of the things, her and Jax took everything up to her room. By the time they came back downstairs, I had the table set so we could eat.

"Damn, Sasha, this food hitting, I forgot your ass could cook," Jax said, making me blush.

"Thanks, babe," I said. Shit with Jaxen has been hot and heavy over the last few weeks and I was enjoying every damn moment of it. Jayla also seemed to be much happier about having Jaxen around more often. After dinner was over, I gave Jayla her bath and put her down for bed. When I walked back downstairs, Jaxen was in his phone texting. He was so into it that he didn't even hear me come down the stairs. I knew he was texting a bitch because Jaxen didn't text with niggas, especially nothing deep. Now I was in my feelings about it.

"Really, Jaxen?" I asked, standing in front of him with my hands on my hips.

"Sasha, what the hell are you talking about now?" He quizzed.

"I know you're texting one of your bitches. You deep into the phone that you didn't even hear me come down the stairs."

"Sasha, don't start your shit. I'm a single fucking man and can text whomever I please. I don't question you so don't question me!" Jax yelled, crushing my feelings. I didn't know why I let him get to me the way I do.

"But you're in my house doing this shit, Jaxen. That's so disrespectful," I told him.

"Sasha, I pay every fucking bill in this house, so don't come at me with no shit like that, you know what I'm the fuck out, I was about to bless you with this dick but that's what got you acting simple now," Jax stated while getting up to leave.

"Jax is that all I am to you is a piece of ass? Do it even matter to you that I'm the mother of your child? I asked through tears. I loved Jax with everything in me yet I was starting to feel like I was just something to get his dick wet. Jax ran his hands down his face and took a deep breath.

"Sasha, we be good until you start tripping. You can't never let shit be, you always gotta trip and start questioning me. I don't have no wife or no woman. And why wouldn't I care that you have my daughter? Why the hell do you think I brought you this house and pay all the bills? If I didn't care about you, Sasha, I would have just taken my daughter to live with me and not gave a damn where you went. Every time we chilling and having a good time, you want to fuck it up with all this relationship shit. Then when I have to remind you what it is, your ass get all emotional and start crying and shit. Just like you're doing now." I couldn't say shit because Jaxen was right about everything he was saying. I needed to chill and just see where things went.

"You're right, baby. I'm sorry, I don't know why I keep doing that," I told Jaxen, trying to smooth things over.

"I'm serious, Sasha. The next time you bring us up again, I'm just gonna stop fucking with your ass. Now go upstairs and look on the bed, I brought you something."

A big smile appeared on my face because it's been a minute since Jaxen had brought me anything. When I got in the room, on the bed was a pretty white lace lingerie piece. I picked it up to get a good look at it and there was a jewelry box underneath it. I grabbed it with excitement, and I opened the box. It was a tennis bracelet. I was so excited because I knew Jaxen loved me. I knew I wasn't tripping all this time. I walked in the bathroom to freshen up so I could put on Jaxen's gift and gave him the best night of his life.

———

Today was Jayla's birthday and Jaxen and I were throwing her a birthday party at Jaxen's house. Jayla and I both spent the night over here last night, and I was loving the feeling of being a family with him again. It's been about a month since the night he told me to chill, and that's exactly what I was doing. I haven't said a word about us being a couple and everything was working out great. I stopped taking my birth control last week with the hopes of getting pregnant, so I could lock down our family. When I walked downstairs, Jaxen was in the kitchen staring out the window. I walked up behind him and instantly caught an attitude when I saw the way he was staring at the woman that lived next door. It was the same chick I caught him talking to the first time I popped up to his house. It was about the way he acted over her that rubbed me the wrong way. I decided to keep quiet for now and pretend I didn't see him eye-fucking her. Jaxen turned around and faced me once he realized I was in the kitchen

Everything was now set up, the party was starting in a few minutes, and people started to arrive. Since it was finally the beginning of the summertime, we decided to do everything outside. Jaxon hired a BBQ chef to cater Jayla's party, the DJ was set up out back and everything was just perfect. My best friend, Amanda, walked in with gift bags in both hands for Jayla. My baby girl was truly blessed and spoiled at a very young age.

"Where's my god daughter?!" Amanda yelled, making her presence known.

"Stop yelling in my damn house like you're outside," Jaxen said to Amanda. She just rolled her eyes and headed to the backyard. For some reason, Jaxen didn't care too much for Amanda, but I didn't know why. I followed her to the back and found myself a table under the tent. I was ready to just enjoy the party.

Jax came outside a few minutes later only wearing his swim trunks. Jaxen was so damn fine, and if it wasn't for the fact that it was my daughter's party, I would have sucked his dick right there on sight. Jaxen had two pools in his yard, one for the adults and one for the kids. All the kids were outside playing, and the music was bumping. My daughter's party was a success but the only thing I could think about was riding Jax's dick tonight. I had to use the bathroom and when I came outside, I damn near pissed myself when I saw Jax talking to that bitch next door in the yard. I sashayed across the yard until I was standing next to Jaxen, making my presence known.

"Baby, are you ready to sing happy birthday to Jayla?" I asked, being a little shady. Both of them turned to face me and she was wearing the exact look that I wanted her to, but Jax, on the other hand, had a look of disgust on his face.

"Sasha, don't you see me talking? I don't know why you insist on being so fucking rude all the time. I'll be over there in a minute. I'm sorry about that, Zyla." Jaxen turned back around to that bitch, and for some reason, what he said boiled my blood. I knew shit was about to get ugly, but I didn't care 'cause I was sick of Jaxen's shit.

"Are you fucking serious right now, Jaxen? You think you can talk to me anyway that you want just because you talking to this bitch? You got me all the way fucked up, Jax," I snapped. When Jaxen bit his bottom lip before he said anything, I knew that he was pissed, but

I didn't care at that moment. I felt disrespected and both of them was gonna know it.

"Sasha, you outta fucking pocket right now. Why the fuck would you come over here starting shit at your daughter's party just because you saw me talking to my neighbor? This is why we aren't together now because this kinda shit right here," he stated.

"I keep telling you I'm a single fucking man, Sasha and I can do whatever the fuck I want to do. Go ahead with the bullshit before you embarrass yourself more than you already have," he snapped. Jaxen's words cut me deep and the fact that we now had an audience didn't make me feel any better.

"You single, Jaxen? Is that why you've been at my house every fucking night, fucking me for the last few weeks? And didn't I just spend the night here last night fucking you into the wee hours of the night? But you single, right? Go head and keep showing off for this bitch, Jaxen," I yelled.

"Sasha, come on. This is your daughter's party and your embarrassing yourself; don't do this today," Amanda stated and I looked at her like she was crazy. She was supposed to be my best friend, and it felt like she was siding with Jaxen's disrespectful ass.

"Yeah, you need to listen to your best friend," Jaxen said. I couldn't deal with how he was talking to me, so I immediately started swinging on him. My emotions were all over the place, and I knew I probably looked crazy at that point, but my emotions were too far gone to stop.

"Fuck you, Jaxen! How could you treat me like this? I don't deserve this. So you were just using me for sex these last few weeks?" I yelled while swinging on him. I felt someone trying to pull me off him, but I was too wild to be stopped or so I thought. Jaxen grabbed me then shoved me so hard that I flew across the yard.

"Go the fuck home, Sasha! I would never fuck with you like that again. I don't know what I saw in you in the first place. Your ass is crazy. The only reason I started fucking around with you like that again is because you got good pussy, and you know how to suck a dick. Now you know. You need to go home and get yourself together. I'll bring my daughter home in a few days," Jaxen snapped, embarrassing me.

I felt a sharp pain in my chest and it felt like someone had stabbed me in the heart. Jaxen had never spoken to me like that nor had he ever put his hands on me before. I was hurt beyond words, and I could hear people whispering. Some were even laughing. Jaxen's best friend Khi, picked me up from the ground.

"I can't believe that you put your hands on me, Jaxen. You definitely fucked with the wrong bitch heart this time. I got something for your ass, and just so you know I'm fucking pregnant with your second child, you sorry piece of shit!" I yelled and then walked off.

Amanda tried to grab me but I snatched away. "Get the fuck off me, Amanda. You keep dick riding my baby daddy. Yeah, you don't think I know you want Jaxen? Well I do but just know, I would kill both of y'all asses if you tried it."

I walked off deep in my feelings. I didn't see any of the kids outside, so I assumed someone made them go in the house. I didn't even bother to say bye to Jayla, I just got in my car and cried my heart out. I felt like a fucking failure because I ruined my daughter's party. I knew I shouldn't have lied about being pregnant, but I knew that would fuck Jaxen up. Eventually, I got myself together, pulled off, and headed home. Once I got in the house, I laid on the couch and cried myself to sleep.

S hit has been pretty good between me and Mark. He's been coming home right after work and spending most of his time at home with me and Zoey. I had to fall back from Jaxen because shit was starting to get heated with us, and I knew if I would have kept spending time with him, eventually, I would have bust it open. Although Jaxen and I weren't spending time together, I couldn't help but think about him all the time. Jaxen and I shared a chemistry that I didn't have with Mark. I loved my husband to death, but we didn't have that magical feeling that I felt when I was with Jaxen. I saw his daughter and her mother at his house a little more than usual. Even though Jaxen told me that he would never be with her again, I could tell that she was in love with him. Which meant he was probably still fucking her from time to time. I couldn't front if I wanted to, but I hated seeing her over there with him. I knew I didn't have a right to feel no type of way, but I did. Especially since I was supposed to be making it work with my husband. I was really feeling some type of way when I saw that she spent the night with him. I was in my yard watering my garden when Jaxen walked over and started talking to me.

"Wassup, Zyla? You know I miss you, right? But I guess I have to respect the fact that you decided to work things out with your wack ass husband," Jaxen stated sarcastically.

"I see you decided to work things out with Jayla's mom," I shot back.

"I see your ass got jokes. She's only here because today is Jayla's birthday party, if you must know. Why don't you bring Zoey over to the party? She would have a ball and she can bring a swimsuit. Hell, you could bring one too."

"Well, Zoey is with my parents this weekend so she won't be able to attend the party," I told him. Before Jaxen had a chance to respond, his baby mom walked up to tell him it was time to sing happy birthday, and from there, all hell broke loose. I was just looking until she called me a bitch. I let the first time slide, but I was ready to fuck her up by the third time. However, I didn't have a chance to say anything with the way Jaxen and her were going at it.

My heart damn near dropped out of my chest when she said that her and Jaxen had been fucking for the last few weeks and that she was just fucking him last night. I walked away from the yard and let them handle their business because I couldn't stand to hear any more about their love affair. I knew I had no right to be upset about what he did with her, but for some reason, I just couldn't help but feel some type of way.

After I turned away, I made my way into the house. As soon as I hit the living room, Mark was standing there staring at me with so much anger in his eyes. I knew he must have saw me talking to Jax. I cursed myself out because I should have known better, but I thought Mark was still sleeping.

"So, you still talking to that hoodlum, Zyla?" Mark asked while walking in my space.

"Mark, don't start. You know I'm here with you ninety-nine percent of the time, so don't fucking start because you saw me talking to Jax. We've been doing so good, Mark so there is no need for you to be insecure. Besides, my husband is all the man I need," I assured him while pulling him in for a hug. To my surprise, he returned the favor, and it felt so good.

Once Mark and I pulled apart from each other, he kissed my forehead then sat down on the couch. I knew deep down inside he had a feeling that something was going on, but he couldn't deny the truth about us being together all the time. Mark was even working from home as much as he could. I made my way into the kitchen, so I could make us both something to eat. When I walked over to my sink, I could see Jax's back yard, and all of the kids were having so much fun. A smile crept up on my face, but when the thought of his baby mama being pregnant came to mind, I got upset instantly. Then I brushed it off and continued to fix me and my husband some lunch.

———

THE FEELING OF ZOEY TAPPING ME WOKE ME UP FROM MY well-needed nap. It was Sunday and Mark, and I had been fucking all over the house all weekend long. I needed a nap since I started class tomorrow. Mark didn't act like he was too pleased with it, but he knew it was something I had dreamed about for some time now. I was going to do it regardless if I had his blessing or not.

"Hey, my princess! What you doing here?" I cooed at Zoey.

"Hey, mama. Daddy picked me up from nana and pop pop's house. We had so much fun over there, but I missed you too." Zoey smiled, kissing my cheek.

"Aww, baby, I miss you more. Where is your daddy at?"

"He told me to keep you up here while he takes all the food out of the containers. He wanted you to think he cooked, but he really didn't, Nana sent some food over." We both laughed as I peeled my tired body from the bed. I went to go see what my crazy ass husband was up to.

"Ok, baby. Let mama get cleaned up and you go help daddy finish up the surprise. Don't tell him you told me the truth, okay?"

Zoey ran off while I made my way into the bathroom. I washed my face and brushed my teethe then headed downstairs with my family. When I got to the kitchen, Mark had put the food on plates and all I could do was laugh since I knew that he didn't actually cook the food. When I sat at the table, she winked at me then giggled. I winked back and we just let Mark shine for the night. It was such a good feeling spending the evening with my baby and my husband.

The day I took Jayla home, Sasha and I got into it again. Now I was sitting on my couch in my feelings because her crazy ass hasn't been letting me see my damn daughter. I had been trying to catch up with her for the past couple of weeks, but she's been on good bullshit. So, since she was playing Petty Betty, I had some shit for her dumb ass. Khi and I was about to head over there as soon as he pulled up. I was so done with Sasha. Then she gone try to say that pregnant shit in front of Zyla, pissing me off even more. I could tell by the way Zyla face turned up she was hurt by hearing Sasha say that dumb shit. I also knew baby girl was still feeling me. I respected her for trying to work shit out with her husband, but after all the shit he has done to her that nigga didn't need a chick like Zyla. She was a good girl, and if he fucked up again, I would for sure be right there to pick up the pieces. The knock at my door bought me out of my thoughts. I jumped up to answer it because I knew it was Khi. I opened the door and he looked like he had a lot on his mind.

"What's good with you, bro?" I asked a little concerned.

"Man, remember that chick Kia I was fucking."

"Yeah, I remember. What about her?"

"She pregnant and she just started showing out of nowhere. Man, I ain't trying to have no baby by that hoe. She was just a good fuck and she would only call me when her man was with his wife. I was happy as fuck she had somebody, but when he started acting like he wanted to be the happy husband, she started getting lonely again. I asked her was the seed mine, and she said no."

"So, what's the problem if she said no?"

"I just don't need her trying to put that shit on me when baby boy goes back home with his wife. Not to mention if she was fucking me and him raw, there could be somebody else. I just don't need the drama, bro," Khi expressed.

Khi enjoyed his single life with no kids, so I knew this shit was bothering him. Don't get me wrong, my boy talked about having kids. He just wasn't ready for all that right now. He said he wanted to be retired from the street life and sitting on more money than he could handle with a bad ass wife on his arm, then he would work on the babies. Khi was very adamant about that.

"Man, listen. For starters, you should have been using something with that hoe. Secondly, let that shit go. If it comes up later that the baby is yours, then you do something about it. Until then, it ain't yours. Now, if you see the baby somewhere later on and it looks like you, get that test done. Or just get it done asap so you won't be stressing over it."

"Maybe I will do that, but enough about my shit. You ready to ride out?"

"Yup, let's do this. I'ma grab my phone and house key then we can be out."

Since Khi had a new whip, we were going to get in his shit and head to Sasha's house since she been ignoring me. I wanna see my daughter, and she's not going to keep her away from me because she's feeling some type of way. This is one of the reasons I shouldn't have started fucking with her ass. I was laying up, sucking, fucking, and giving her hope when I knew what we once had was a done deal. We were doing good co-parenting until I was thinking with my little head instead of my big one. Usually, I would be strong enough to keep it moving, but seeing Zyla trying to make shit work with her husband got to me. I didn't wanna sleep alone every night and now look at what this shit got me.

Khi and I hopped in his car and headed to Sasha's house. I planned on sitting right outside, down the block and wait for her evil ass to show up. Khi and I were only sitting in the car for about a half hour before Sasha crazy ass pulled up. While she was getting Jayla out the car, Khi and I walked up on her ass.

"Daddy!" Jayla yelled out in excitement. I was so happy to see my baby girl. Sasha was mean mugging me, but I didn't give a fuck. I knew some shit was about to go down with Sasha and I, so I sent Jayla to the car with Khi.

"Hey, princess. Daddy missed you so much, so I'm gonna take you with me for a few days. Go get in the car with Uncle Khi while I talk to mommy for a minute." Sasha was about to object, but I gave her a look that stopped her right in her tracks.

"Okay, daddy. Bye, mommy," Jayla said and then walked off with Khi. As soon as Jayla was down the street, I turned my attention to Sasha's dumb ass.

"Have you lost your motherfucking mind keeping my daughter away from me? Sasha, I swear you really fucking testing me, and I can assure you that's not what you want to do. This isn't a fucking game, so don't ever play with me when it comes to my daughter. You will lose every damn time and don't think running to my G-mom is gonna help your ass," I threatened.

"Who the hell do you think you are, Jaxen? I'm your fucking daughter's mom and was once your woman, and now you wanna treat me like shit?

"The keyword in what you said was once — you're not my fucking girl, Sasha. I'm sorry for making you think otherwise with my actions. I'm a single man, Sasha, and us fucking doesn't change that for one minute. So, I'll never fuck with you like that again and that bullshit you pulled Jayla's party was embarrassing. Why the fuck did you lie and say that you were pregnant? You were foul for that shit."

"Fuck you, Jaxen, and I didn't fucking lie about being pregnant," Sasha shot back.

"I knew you would say that shit, so I'm about to see for myself. Let's go," I said, grabbing her by the arm.

"Jaxen, get the hell off me! And what do you mean you about to find out for yourself?" She asked, trying to snatch her arm away. I was tired of playing with Sasha, so I picked her ass up, carried her to the front door, and used my key to open the door. Of course she was being extra and screaming for me to put her down. As soon as we got in the house, I pulled out a pregnancy test, and the look on Sasha's face told me everything I needed to know. I knew right then and there her ass was for sure lying.

"Go in the bathroom and take this test, Sasha. I want you to make a liar out of me." Sasha snatched the test from my hand and walked to the bathroom. I sat in the living room and waited for her to come out. When she walked out the bathroom and handed me the pregnancy test, I looked down at the test and my heart damn near stop beating. That bitch was telling the truth.

"I told your dumb ass I wasn't lying, now please get the fuck out of my house," Sasha yelled.

"I don't know how you got that test to say positive, but I know your ass ain't pregnant," I told her. Something in my gut was telling me that she wasn't pregnant. Yeah, I was fucking her on the regular, but I made sure I was extra careful to prevent getting her pregnant.

"You sound dumb as hell, Jaxen. Just get out!" she yelled.

I didn't even bother to argue with her, I just walked out and slammed the door behind me. I hoped like hell that test was a mistaken because there was no way I was about to raise another child with her simple ass.

The ride back to my house was silent because I was fucked up. I could tell that Khi knew something was wrong, but he didn't say shit because Jayla was in the car. After stopping pass McDonald's, we headed back to my house. When we pulled up, Zyla and her punk ass husband were walking into their home. She was looking damn good in the white one-piece short set she had on. I was just pissed that she was with that clown ass nigga. As soon as we walked in the house, Khi started with the questions.

"Yo' what happen with you and Sasha that got you all zoned out? You've been quiet ever since we left her crib."

"You remember at Jayla's party when Sasha said she was pregnant? Well, I asked her ass why did she lie, and she gonna tell me that she didn't lie, so I made her ass take a test and that shit came back positive. But I know in my gut that it's some bullshit. I made sure I was extra careful not to get her pregnant. I'm gonna get to the bottom of this shit, but I don't know what the hell I'm gonna do if that bitch is really pregnant. I don't want to deal with her ass now," I told Khi, who just shook his head.

"Damn, you sounding like me right now, but you never know. These broads are slimy as hell. Did Sasha take the test in front of you?"

"Nah, I was in the living room."

"Make her ass take that shit again and stay in the bathroom with her. I think I'm about to get a DNA test while Kia ass is still pregnant because I don't want know surprises."

"I feel you and don't worry, I'm definitely making her ass retake that test," I told Khi. A couple of minutes went by and Khi left, so Jayla and I sat on the couch chilling and watching TV for the rest of the night.

The next morning when Jayla and I woke up, I decided to take my baby girl out to eat breakfast then we headed over to my grandma's house. As soon as we walked in the door, my G-mom hugged Jayla tightly and placed kisses over her small cheeks.

"How's grandma's baby doing?" My G-mom asked her.

"I'm good, nana. Me and my dad just came back from eating pancakes," Jayla revealed.

"You should have come here for some of my famous pancakes

because IHOP don't have anything on my pancakes," my G-mom boasted. I couldn't lie, my favorite old lady's food be hitting. If she was to open up her own restaurant, she would put most of these niggas out of business.

"Oooh, can I stay the night so you can make me some in the morning?"

"You sure can, pudding. Now go play in your room so I can talk to your father." Jayla ran off upstairs and I wondered what the hell G-mom wanted. I had a feeling she was about to start her bullshit.

"What's up, G-mom?"

"Sasha called me and told me what you did to her. If you claim you didn't want to be with her, why the hell would you keep fucking the girl? Now she's carrying your second child. You need to just go ahead and marry that girl, Jaxen."

"I would never marry that crazy ass girl, and I wish you stop listening to everything that Sasha tells you. That girl is a liar. I know she's lying about being pregnant so I'm not paying that girl any damn mind. Now, if you don't mind. I would appreciate if you stay out of my personal business concerning her unless I come to you. I wish you would stop taking the word of her over your own flesh and blood."

"Boy, I don't know who the hell you think you're talking to like that, but you're not too old to get your ass kicked up in here. If you would have kept your dick in your pants, you wouldn't have to worry about if she was telling the truth or not. And I heard about you fucking around with that married tramp from next door," my grandma stated. It was something about her calling Zyla a tramp that pissed me off.

"G-mom, I love you and all, but you really need to chill the hell out. You're talking shit about something you don't know shit about. You keep listening to Sasha's bitter ass. As a matter of fact, since you love her hoe ass so much, maybe you should be with her!" I yelled. I knew that I fucked up when I said that, but I was tired of this bullshit with Sasha.

Whap!

I couldn't believe that my grandma had just slapped me in my face. It took everything in me not to slap her ass back. I knew I had to get out of there and quick before I did or said something that I would forever regret. I stood there holding my face for a few seconds before I made my exit.

"I'm done with this shit, but don't ever put your hands on me again. And since you care so much about Sasha, you let her take care of you. Please don't bother to call me. You can have her come pick up Jayla when she's ready to go home," I retorted before storming out the door.

I hopped in my car, mad as hell. I was ready to go choke the shit out of Sasha, but I decided against it because I knew I would have killed her ass right then and there. I was starting to hate Sasha, and I regretted fucking with her more and more every day that went by. Sasha was dumb as hell if she thought for one moment that her behavior was going to make me want her. The one thing I did know was if she was pregnant and she had the baby, I was gonna take both of them from her dumb ass. I pulled off and headed to the hood. I needed a drink or two with the way I was feeling so I decided to go to Luby's bar. When I sat down, I ordered a double shot of Henny, which turned into three double shots within in the hour. I was fucked up and I knew I couldn't drive home. I dialed Khi's number, but he didn't answer, so I called the only other number I could think of.

"Hello?" Zyla's sweet voice answered on the second ring.

"Zyla, I need you to come pick me up. I'm fucked up right now and I can't drive," I slurred into the phone.

"Jaxen, why the hell would you call me of all people? I can't come pick you up, but I can call you a cab.

"Come on, Zyla! Just come pick me up? What your punk ass husband sitting in your face?"

"Jaxen, you're being disrespectful, and I'm hanging up," Zyla said before disconnecting the call. I was so pissed that I called back, but she didn't answer. I heard my phone ring, and when I looked at the phone. it was Khi calling back.

"Yo', what's up? Khi asked.

"I need you to come get me from Luby's; I can't drive." Khi let out a heavy sigh before speaking.

"Aight, man. I'll be there."

———

THE NEXT MORNING WHEN I WOKE UP, MY HEAD WAS POUNDING, and I felt like shit. Even though I had a hangover, I remembered everything that happened yesterday, including the fact that I called Zyla being disrespectful. I knew I had to apologize to her because that wasn't cool at all. As far as my grandma and Sasha, I didn't have shit to say to either of them no time soon. Once I was finished handling my hygiene, I grabbed my phone, so I could text Zyla.

Me: Good morning, Zyla. I just wanted to apologize about last night cause I was out of pocket. I was just going through something and I wanted to see you but I went about it the wrong way

Zyla: Good morning, Jaxen. Yes, you were out of pocket. Just don't let that happen again. Luckily, Mark wasn't at home when you called, but listen if you need to talk, we can talk a little later since Mark is going out of town for a couple of days. Just no funny business, we need to keep it respectful.

Me: I promise I'll keep it respectful. I can't lie and say I don't miss your sexy ass though.

Zyla replied with an angry face and I just laughed. Although I really liked Zyla and wanted her for myself, she and I had really become pretty close friends. At one point, we were spending time together almost every damn day. I went through my phone and seen that I had missed calls from my G-mom and Sasha, but I didn't plan to call either of them back. My G-mom and I had never had this type of falling out before, but I was tired of her coming at me over Sasha. I was sick of Sasha running to G-mom every time her and I got into it. I decided to get dressed and get with Khi for a few hours. I wished I was in some pussy, if I could be honest. I had options, but I wasn't feeling none of them like that. I wanted to feel the inside of Zyla like yesterday, but the way shit was looking, I didn't see that happening anytime soon if ever.

It's been a little over a month since Jaxen made me take a pregnancy test, which I knew he would do and that's exactly why I had paid a pregnant woman a hundred dollars for her piss. I was just glad that we were at my house at the time or my ass would have been caught in my lie. Jaxen's grandma told me that they got into it and he wasn't fucking with either of us right now. I was starting to regret lying to Jaxen about being pregnant. It was too much work to keep the lie up. On top of that, he wasn't even talking to me. When he wanted to talk to Jayla, he called the cell phone that he brought for her, and when he wanted to see her, he would have Khi pick her up. Jaxen's grandma had called me last night and asked if I could stop by while Jayla was in school so we could talk. After I dropped Jayla off, I headed straight over to Jaxen's grandma's crib. I knocked on the door and she opened the door on the first knock.

"Hey, Grandma Pam. How are you?" I greeted Jaxen's grandma.

"Hey, baby. I'm okay just missing my grandson like crazy. I know I smacked him, but boy, is he pretty pissed with me. We've never went without speaking and my little heart just can't take it anymore," Grandma Pam stated sadly. I instantly felt bad since all of this was my fault.

"He'll come around, Grandma Pam. You know he's a stubborn man," I told her.

"Yeah, I know. He gets that from his mother. Anyway, I didn't call you all this way to discuss him. I called you here because I need a big favor from you?"

"Anything. What can I help you with?"

"I need you to take this pregnancy test. Jaxen swears there's no way he could have gotten you pregnant and me taking up for you is the reason why my grandson isn't fucking with me right now," she stated. My heart was in my stomach because I didn't see that shit coming from her but I knew I was caught. I didn't know what to say. I couldn't take that test right now because I didn't have the piss with me. I stayed silent for a moment trying to think of something to say.

"I actually don't have to pee right now; I just went to the bath-room before I got here," I told her.

"So, he was right. All this time I thought you were a nice girl, but I can see now that you're exactly who he said you were. I feel like a damn fool right now. Sasha, why would you tell such a lie?" She quizzed. I started crying because I knew I had fucked up, so I might as well tell her the truth.

"I'm sorry, I know I shouldn't have lied. It's just I love Jaxen so much, and I felt like I was losing him. When I first said I was preg-nant, I only said it to be smart, but I guess I took things too far. I even paid someone for their pee. I just want to be with Jaxen more than anything," I cried.

"Sasha, do you know how dumb you sound? Did you think lying to him and trying to force him to be with you was gonna work? You must don't know Jaxen at all. It was one thing to lie to him, but it was another to lie to me. I'll never trust another word that you say. Honestly, I really think that you should leave. I can't stand to look at you right now," she stated harshly.

Her words cut me deep and caused me to cry even harder. She was right about everything she said. I was a fool to think that I could get Jaxen to be with me based off a lie. I got up and headed towards the door. I was so embarrassed that I couldn't even look her way.

"I'm really sorry about all of this. I really am," I apologized again before walking out the door.

When I got home, I called Amanda because I really needed someone to talk to. Even though I haven't talked to her since the day I showed my ass at my daughter's party. Amanda had been calling and leaving messages, but I wasn't ready to talk to her until now.

"Hello," I cried into the phone when Amanda answered the phone.

"Sasha, what's wrong?"

"I messed up, Amanda! I need you to come over," was all I said.

"I'll be right there," Amanda said before disconnecting the line.

When Amanda got there, I told her what the hell I did. And just like typical Amanda, instead of being the friend that I needed, she told me what I already knew.

"Sasha, I keep telling you time and time again that you need to let Jaxen go. You don't wanna hear that from me, but you two are toxic together."

"Amanda, why the fuck can't you just be a friend and listen to me for a change? All you ever do is tell me what I need to be doing. I just needed you to be a listening ear, that's all. Nothing more, nothing less," I vented because I didn't need anyone to tell me what I did was wrong.

"You seem to be a little obsessed with Jaxen, Sasha, and that shit isn't healthy at all. It's like when it comes to him, you get weak as shit. I would never wanna be that weak over no nigga. Especially one that don't even want you no more. I know you hate my realness, but what type of friend would I be if I didn't say shit?" Amanda said, continuing to piss me the hell off. I know I called her, but I instantly regretted it. Every time we talked about Jax, Amanda had me side-eying her. I knew in my heart that Amanda wanted Jaxen for herself.

"Why every time we talk you Team Jax? When are you going to admit that you want my baby daddy, Amanda? I mean, for years, you've been Team Jax, and the crazy part is he don't even like ya ass. So, what's the real deal? Have you been jealous of us for all these years?"

"Wooh, bitch. Yeah, you don' lost all the sense that God done gave you. First of all, Jax is not my type, never have been. I don't do street niggas, and if you were a true friend, you would know my type. I only came over here to be here for you, and here you go attacking me with this bullshit. You know what? My god daughter knows my number, have her call me if she needs me. I'm gone get out of here." I guess I struck a nerve with Amanda because I never saw her this mad at me. I guess everybody was fed up with my shit. Once I heard my front door shut, I made my way into the kitchen to grab my bottle of wine then headed back to the living room to sit on my couch to drink my sorrows away.

It was now mid-September but it was already starting to get cold outside. I was in the house making dinner after a long day of school. Everything with me and Mark was going good... besides the fact that I was almost sure that I had fallen in love with Jaxen. I loved my husband, but that spark just wasn't there anymore. I honestly didn't know what to do when it came to my husband. I would feel crazy for leaving him now when he's doing everything right. The smell of my seafood alfredo had the house smelling like love.

"Mommy, are you making Garlic bread too?" Zoey asked in her sweet voice.

"Of course, I am. Who eats alfredo without garlic bread?" I told her, placing a kiss on her cheek. Zoey ran off to play while I finished up with dinner. Dinner had just got done and like clockwork, Mark was walking in the door from work. I felt Mark's arms wrap around my waist, followed by a kiss on the back of my neck.

"Hey, baby. It's smelling good as hell in here. How was school?"

"School was good. I have a paper to do for homework. How was work?"

"Work was long. I have to leave to go to New York on Friday, but I'll be home Sunday morning," Mark revealed. I knew I was wrong, but the first thought that came to mind was I would be able to see Jaxen without risking getting caught. The only reason I even tried to avoid him was because I was trying to avoid giving him some pussy. I wanted to feel Jaxen inside of me so badly. After we finished eating dinner, I washed the dishes while Mark put Zoey to bed. Since I was so horny, I knew it was gonna go down. Just as I thought, as soon as I made it out the shower, Mark threw me on the bed and started feasting on my sweet spot that led up to two hours of lovemaking.

Two days later...

Last night Mark and I had a wonderful night, but his phone had been going off all night long. Things had been going good between us, so I didn't wanna start assuming shit, especially when I was doing my dirt too. I just kept it to myself so I wouldn't start no shit. Plus, he was about to go on a business trip, so that could have been one of his coworkers. Hell, or even his boss, so I just pushed the shit to the back of my head.

"Good Morning, beautiful," Mark said, walking into the kitchen. He sat at the table and I handed him a blueberry muffin and a cup of coffee while I ran to grab Zoey.

"Come on, pretty mama. Let's get up, so you can get you some cereal." I was up extra early this morning, so Zoey was already dressed. I hurried and put her clothes on while she slept peacefully, so she just needed to eat and brush her teeth. I sent her in the bathroom while I ran to my bedroom to get something.

"Mama, daddy phone was laying on the sink and it was ringing. I answered it and the lady told me to get my daddy." I looked at the phone and it said, Keese.

"Hello," I said, and there was no response, but breathing could be heard.

"Hello," I said again and then the person hung up. I just slid the phone in my pocket and made my way downstairs with Zoey following behind me. When we made it to the kitchen, Mark was getting up from the table.

"Baby, did you see my phone?" He asked with a puzzled look on his face.

"Yes, daddy. The lady said to put you on the phone."

"What lady, baby?" Mark asked with big eyes.

"When I looked at the phone, I saw the name Keese, so I thought maybe he sounded like a girl. When I said hello, he hung up," I said, handing him the phone. I knew it was some weird shit going on, but like I said before, I was going to let it go.

"Oh, that's the new coworker. Thanks for grabbing it for me, baby. I'm going to go ahead and head out, and remember I'm heading to New York straight from work. So, when I get there and get settled, I'ma call you."

"Ok, I love you and be safe," I said, not really being able to contain my excitement. Mark was going to be gone and I was going to have the weekend to spend with Jax.

It was late Friday evening and Mark had just Face timed me to let me know that he made it to New York safely. After talking for a few, we finally hung up. I went to my car to grab some paperwork that I left in there.

"That's a nice view," I heard Jaxen say from behind me. I couldn't help but smile at his comment.

"Thanks. I'm glad to know that you're enjoying the view," I flirted back. It was something about Jaxen that made me tingly on the inside. I was about to say something else until I heard Melissa's annoying ass mouth.

"Hello, Jaxen. You're looking good as usual." Melissa flirting Jax angered me for some reason, but I had to keep my cool. "Oh hey, Zyla," she spoke sarcastically.

"Hey, Melissa. What brings you on this side of the street?" I asked with an eye roll.

"Oh, just this fine, single man right here," Melissa stated, smiling hard as hell.

"Melissa, who said anything about me being single?"

"Trust me, you're single. Besides your baby mama, I have never seen another woman over here before," she stated, sounding like a stalker.

"You may haven't seen another woman here before but just know that my heart belongs to someone else, so that makes me unavailable," he stated while looking me dead in my eyes. It was something about the way Jaxen said that his heart was already taken that had me hot and bothered.

"Anyway ladies, I have to get going. I holla at you later, Zyla," Jaxen said before hopping in his car.

"I never thought I'd see the day when you would be fucking around on your husband with the hot neighbor."

"Melissa, you really need to get a life. I'm not you, messing around on my husband is not something that I do. Unlike you, I'm very aware that I'm married, and I take my vows seriously. Now, if you don't mind, I have more important things to do with my time," I told her before walking away.

The truth is I was in my feelings because, in a way, Melissa was right. I was messing around on Mark with Jaxen. I may not have been fucking him, but I do sneak around to see and talk to him behind my husband's back, we've kissed and went on a few dates. I really have to figure this shit out. I was really in a tough spot. I loved my husband, and I was in love with Jaxen, but I knew that I could never break up my family to be with him.

Zoey deserved to have a two-parent home and I would never be able to live with myself knowing that I would be the cause of her losing her family. I swear shit was much easier when Mark was out doing his own thing, I felt like I was in the right to start something with Jaxen, but now that Mark was doing everything right and more, I'm not sure what I wanna do anymore. I'm so confused. This shit is crazy. I just made my way back into the house and waited for Jax to call me later on because I knew he would as soon as he made it back in the house.

. . .

Knock Knock

Someone knocking at my door woke me up from my deep slumber and when I looked over at the clock, it was barely 9 a.m. Jaxen and I ended up talking on the phone damn near all night. The call was intense and made me feel good and bad at the same time. Jaxen always expressed his feelings for me, but this time it was different. Jaxen was raw and put his heart on the line, which also led me to open up and express my true feelings about him. When we hung up, I went to bed, but I tossed and turned for the rest of the night due to Jax being on my brain. Which led to me having a terrible night. I had just gotten to sleep like five this morning. Now here it is somebody banging on my damn door.

I GOT UP WITH AN ATTITUDE AND HEADED TO THE DOOR. WHEN I snatched the door open, I was ready to curse out whoever was knocking at my door like the damn police.

"Well damn, what's the attitude for? You knew I was coming back into town this weekend. I've been missing you and my god daughter so much. You knew as soon as I got to town, I was coming over here early in the morning, so you might as well get your ass up because we're going to breakfast," my best friend, Tasia, said all in one breath. I had forgot all about her coming back this weekend.

"Tasia, you could have called me instead of banging on my damn door like the cops."

"Girl, please. Like you would have answered. Get dressed, I'm starving," Tasia demanded. I just waived her off and went back to my room to get dressed. Forty-five minutes later, we headed out the door.

"Just so you know you're driving," I told her.

"Okay, but you're paying," Tasia shot back. I just shook my head and got into the passenger side of her car. It was just like Tasia to wake me up out of my sleep then make me bring her to breakfast. Twenty minutes later, we pulled up to IHOP in Cherry Hill.

"I can't wait to stuff my face, I'm hungry as shit," Tasia stated as the hostess walked us to our seat. "Wait. Where the hell is my god daughter at?" Tasia's ghetto ass yelled.

"Zoey is with my parents; she's actually been spending every other weekend over there with them. I'm surprised that she likes it there especially with my bougie ass mom. I could see why she likes being with my dad."

"Well, that's good, so how's shit been with you and your crazy ass husband?" I sighed heavily before answering her question.

"Honestly, Tasia, Mark is doing everything that I should be doing and more, but my heart just isn't with Mark anymore. I done fucked around and fell in love with Jaxen. I haven't had sex with him, that is about the only thing that we haven't done. But I want him so bad that I might as well be fucking him because I fantasize about him day and night."

"Damn girl, that's some serious shit. So what are you going to do?"

"That's the problem, I don't know what to do. Zoey deserves to have a two-parent family home, and I would hate to be the cause of robbing her of that especially since Mark isn't even doing shit wrong anymore. I feel like I would be no better than him if I gave into Jaxen," I told Tasia honestly.

"Girl, I can't lie. I don't know shit about being married and having a family of my own. I will say this, although Mark might be doing his best now, the damage that he has already done is too severe to ignore. The heart knows what it wants. Just make sure that if you do leave Mark, make sure it's because you want out because it's too broke to fix and not because you're lusting over a man that's giving you the twenty percent that Mark isn't giving you. All I'm saying is if you leave him, make sure it's because you're done, but don't leave him for another man. And no matter what choice you make, Zoey will be just fine," Tasia stated. I just nodded my head in agreement because she was right about everything that she said.

"Good morning, Zyla." When I looked up, I was looking into the eyes of the man that had my life in such a confused state.

"Good morning, Jaxen," I spoke shyly. Tasia eyes got wide as she looked Jaxen and the guy that he was standing with, up and down.

"Oh my, both of you are fine. I'm Tasia, Zyla's best friend. It's finally a pleasure to meet you, Jaxen," Tasia spoke, holding out her hand for Jaxen to shake. "And who might you be?" she asked the guy he was with and Jaxen was smiling hard as hell at Tasia's crazy ass.

"I'm Khi, and I'm Jaxen's best friend. It's a pleasure to meet both of you."

"Why don't you gentlemen join us, we were just about to order?" Tasia's big mouth said. I wasn't sure that was a good idea.

"Aight cool," Jaxen said. They sat down, we all ordered our food and indulged in basic conversation. I could tell that Tasia was feeling Khi. I couldn't lie, he was definitely nice looking with a pretty smile, he could dress his ass off, and he could hold a good conversation.

I kept feeling like somebody was staring at me, so I finally looked up and noticed two women, staring at me. One was visibly pregnant, but I didn't know who either of them was so I continued eating and talking. Khi and Tasia flirted with one another while Jaxen and I comfortably eye-fucked one another like it was just the two of us at the table.

"I can see why your ass is so in love with his ass; y'all chemistry is crazy," Tasia blurted, making this shit even more awkward than it already was. Just as I was about to respond, the two women that had been staring at me, were now standing at our table, catching everyone's attention.

"Well hello, Khi," the pregnant girl spoke, sarcastically.

"Wassup, Kia?" Khi spoke.

"Nothing much, just came to feed my baby," she stated while rubbing her stomach, but for some reason she was staring at me, and I was about ready to curse her ass out.

"Khi, stop looking so worried. How many times do I have to tell you that this isn't your baby? My baby belongs to someone else, trust me." And I swear she cut her eye at me again.

"If you don't mind, we're trying to enjoy our breakfast. So, if you're finished with your little reunion, could you please leave our table?" Tasia blurted.

"Excuse me?" the other girl chimed in.

"Are you deaf? It is rude to come to someone's table and hold a full conversation with someone that you clearly see is out with someone else. And no one asked you whose baby that was so stop being tacky. How you know he wanted anyone to know he fucked your ghetto ass?" Tasia snapped. The girl was about to say something else until the pregnant girl Kia smiled and pulled the other girl's arm telling her to just leave it alone. Surprisingly, the girl listened, and they both left the restaurant.

After the ghetto girls left, Khi explained that he used to fuck around with the girl Kia, but we figured that much out when she told him it wasn't his baby. After talking a little longer, Khi paid the bill. Tasia and Khi exchanged numbers before Tasia and I headed back to my house. No sooner then I got in the car, my phone rang, and it was Mark Face timing me.

"Hello?" I answered, happily, but Mark was wearing a scowl on his face.

"Where the fuck are you at?" Marked asked angrily.

"I'm in the car with Tasia; we just left IHOP. What the fuck is your problem?"

"You're my fucking problem. You wanna tell me why my wife is out on a double fucking date while I'm out of town working?

"Mark, I don't know who the fuck you're getting your informa tion from, but I wasn't on no damn double date. But if you must know the neighbor and his friend walked in, and since it turned out that Tasia and his friend was cool, she invited them to sit with us. I don't have to lie to you, but who the fuck is all up in my damn business that felt like they needed to call you to report what I'm doing?" I yelled.

"How I know ain't important. If you weren't out here acting single, it wouldn't be anything to report. I have a meeting, but I'll deal with this shit when I'm done!" Mark yelled before hanging up, never giving me a chance to say anything. I was so pissed that I called back, but his ass sent me to voicemail.

I was now on my way headed home with so much shit on my mind. Zyla was on some sneaky shit and Kia was on some stalking shit. I had been doing everything to keep Zyla happy, and leaving Kia alone was one of them. Now out of the blue, this girl kept blowing my phone up, leaving notes on my windshield. Kia was on some crazy shit, and if she kept it up, I was going to put my foot in her ass. My phone going off let me know that I had a text message. I hoped to God it wasn't Kia ass.

Wifey: Can you please stop at Walmart when you get back in Jersey? I got into studying and forgot we needed some things.

Me: Just send me the list of what you need.

Wifey: Ok...thank you. I love you.

Zyla texted back and I didn't respond. I just threw my phone back into the passenger seat and continued driving. I would look at the list when I got to Walmart. I had been going on these business trips for the past couple of weeks, and I was growing tired of it. My boss had been on the bullshit lately. I did meet me a bad chick over in New York, but I couldn't enjoy her without Kia blowing me up. When she called me and told me about Zyla being in IHOP with that gangster, my blood was boiling. Then when she described Zyla ghetto ass best friend, I was even more pissed. Tasia, Zyla and I go way back. We all went to school together, but I didn't like Tasia because she was always up in our business. Zyla thought she was slick, but we were going to talk about this when I got back home.

An hour later, I was pulling up in the Walmart parking lot. I grabbed my wallet out of the glove compartment and my phone out of the passenger seat, then made my way into the store. I opened up my phone and looked at the long list she sent and started to shake my head. The first thing on the list pissed me off because she knows I hated grabbing pads and tampons. I grabbed a shopping cart then headed to the feminine product aisle.

When I got to the aisle, my eyes locked on this chick that was bent over. She had on a sports bra and a pair of tights like she had just come from the gym. What I needed was on the other side of her. I tried to squeeze by her without bumping her, but when she stood up, she bumped me.

"Oh, I'm sorry. I didn't even see you."

"You're fine, sweetheart. I was just trying to get by without bumping into you. I guess one of us was supposed to bump into each other." I chuckled.

"Hmm...you think so?" She asked with a pretty smile. She looked familiar, but I just couldn't place my finger on where I saw her at.

"Yup, I think so. Why else would God have me walking down this aisle? My name is Mark," I said while holding my hand out.

"My name is Sasha...Mark. God probably sent you down here to get your wife some pads since you still wearing that ring," Sasha sassed before turning to walk off. I looked down at my finger pissed that I hadn't taken my ring off like I usually did.

"Wait! Wait, don't go. I know this seems crazy, but my wife left me months ago, and it just hurts, so I still haven't gotten used to not wearing it. She left me for the neighbor." It was like what I had just said made a light go off in her head, but I still saw the sadness in her eyes. I thought to myself, *got her.*

"Wow, I'm sorry to hear that. I guess we both lost the love of our lives to the neighbor," she said with a half-smirk on her face.

"Damn, I'm sorry to hear that, ma. Well, how about we exchange numbers to get to know each other?"

"I would really love that, Mark. I've been really having a hard time, and I could use a friend," she revealed while handing me her phone to put my number in it. Once I was finished, she called me, and I had her number.

"Alright, I got it. I'll be reaching out soon," I said, watching her leave. Once she was out of sight, I hurried, grabbed what Zyla needed, and walked out of the aisle to get everything else I needed. A half hour later, I was heading to my car. Beautiful women were everywhere, and I just couldn't help myself. After I placed everything in the trunk, I shot Zyla a text letting her know I was on my way.

———

"Don't worry about who told me what. I swear if I find out you're dealing with that dude, Zyla, you gone have problems. I been on my shit, being good to you and home all the time. Now you wanna be doing God knows what with that nigga."

"Mark, I wish you lower your fucking voice. I don't know who came to you telling you shit they know nothing about. I already told you Tasia, and I were out to breakfast and she asked them to join us. Nothing more, nothing less. Let me find out you still doing bullshit, that's why you feeling some type of way. You can dish that shit out, but it hurts when it's happening to you. Believe what the fuck you want. I told you what happened," Zyla snapped then walked out of the room.

When I came in, she jumped all over me hugging and kissing me, but I wasn't beat. The shit that Kia called and told me still was on my mind. Kia had been calling me like crazy and I had been ignoring her. The last straw was when she told my daughter to give me the phone. I called her, cursed her ass, and told her that was it for us. Then she called me the next evening telling me that I keep giving her my ass to kiss when my wife was parading around town with a hood nigga. That shit pissed me all the way off. I made her describe who Zyla was with, then I hung up on her ass and called my wife right away.

She had been calling and texting ever since, but I just wasn't for dealing with her nagging ass. Kia's problem is she want me to leave my wife for her and that shit will never happen. My phone going off on the dresser bought me out of my thoughts. I walked over to the dresser and picked it up. When I saw the name Sam pop up, I got excited. I opened the message to see what the hottie I met in Walmart had to say.

Sam: Sorry I'm so late texting you. I couldn't sleep and needed someone to talk to.

Me: You good, ma. I was just laying here not able to sleep. What's good with you?

Sam: Nothing, really just bored and alone. Can I call you?

I knew Zyla was pissed off and she wouldn't be coming back in here, so it only took me a second to tell Sasha I would call her in a second. First, I was going to go downstairs to make sure Zyla was tucked away on the couch. Then I was going to climb back in my bed and give baby girl a call.

I had just come from riding by Jax's house and instantly got angered. The sight that I just had witnessed got under my skin something terrible. I knew we weren't on good terms, but it ain't never took him this long to accept my phone calls. Seeing the neighbor coming out of his house had me so hurt. I had no one to talk to, and I didn't want Jayla to see me crying, so I took her to Jax's grandma's house. She grabbed Jayla and slammed the door in my face. She was still mad with me for lying about being pregnant. After I dropped her off, I made my way home, made me a drink and then laid down. After a while, I got restless and realized that sleep was never going to come. I had too much shit on my mind. I decided to text the dude Mark that I had met in Walmart, and to my surprise, he responded. Now we were on the phone bussin' it up.

"I really enjoyed talking to you tonight."

"I enjoyed talking to you as well. I needed this conversation. Maybe I could get me some sleep now."

"You will. Just remember better days are coming, and it's his loss. Maybe I could take you out this week sometime. My workload be a little hectic, but I'll make some time for you if you're down."

"I'm definitely down, just let me know when you're ready. My daughter is gone most of the time for the weekend with her daddy, so any of those days are good."

"Alright. Well, I'll hit you up tomorrow with the day. It was nice meeting you, Ms. Sasha."

"Ok, and it was nice meeting you as well. Good night, Mark. I'll talk to you soon," I said and then I hung up the phone. Once I laid the phone down, a smile crept up on my face. Mark looked handsome, and from the way he was dressed, I could tell he was a businessman. The more I thought about when I met him, I figured maybe he was what I needed — a change in the type of men.

I've been dealing with hood niggas ever since I started dealing with men. I even flirted with the local block boys when I was little. The shit was crazy, so Mark seemed like a different speed for me. When I heard him say his workload, I was happy to hear he had a real job, so I'm ready to see how this rides out. I still feel some type of way about Jaxen, but maybe I need to get under someone else to get over him. I rolled over and faced the window, hoping to doze off.

FIVE DAYS LATER...

Mark and I had been kicking it on the phone all week. Today was Friday, we were going on our first date, and I couldn't be more excited. We were now pulling up in front of Ms. Tootsie's Soul Food Café over Philly. I had been here before, but years ago. Mark coming around and opening the door for me brought me out of my thoughts.

"Thank you, Mark!" I said, smiling as I got out of the car.

"You're welcome, beautiful," he said, licking his lips.

I decided on a gray halter, maxi dress that had a high split showing off my thigh. It was a nice summer night, so the weather was beautiful. I topped my outfit off with a pair of strappy bling heels and a long, high ponytail that landed at the top of my ass. I knew I looked good and I knew Mark thought the same thing. Once I was outside of the car, and he locked it up, he led the way, placing his hand at the small of my back.

"Hello, I had reservations for two. Mark Holmes is the name."

"Mr. Holmes, you can come right this way. We have a table right in the back near the window like you asked."

Mark and I made it to the back of the restaurant. I was hoping and praying he didn't sit near the band because I wanted us to be able to engage in conversation and able to hear each other. When we made it to the table, Mark pulled the chair out and waited 'til I was seated then pushed it in for me. I was loving all the attention he was giving me. I just hoped it didn't change after we got to know each other.

"Can I get you two something to drink before I leave?" The waitress said while placing the menus in front of us.

"Yes, you could get me a Tropical Blend Tea," I said to the waitress.

"And you can get me a Corona, please," Mark said, still looking at me.

"Ok, and your server Kelly will be back with your drinks," the waitress said.

After the waitress walked off, Mark sat and stared at me for a minute. All I could do was smile. I was so in love with all the attention he was giving me. It had been a long time since I had been out on a date with anyone other than Jaxen. The crazy part was I've never been interested in no one but Jax, but for some reason, I was strongly attracted to Mark. I think it was because we were kind of going through the same thing. Even though I'm not married to Jaxen, my heart was still broke.

"You good over there, beautiful?" Mark asked.

"Yes, just thinking about how much of a gentleman you are. I'm wondering why your wife would wanna leave you. You work, you fine as hell; like what is really going on?" I asked, really wanting to know.

"I just think we grew apart. We've been together since our early teenage years. People do fall out of love, you know. Even though she fell for somebody else, we're still on good terms. I would have never wanted shit to end on bad terms because we have Zoey."

"That's good that y'all stay on good terms for the baby. I wish me and Jax could do that," I said, wishing I didn't say his name. I knew everyone knew who Jax was, good or bad. I hope he let it go and didn't ask any questions.

"Hello, I'm Kelly, your waitress. Here's your drinks. Are you two ready to order?" She asked while sitting our drinks down.

"Yes, please. I will have the smothered turkey chops, baked mac and cheese, and cabbage," I said.

"Let me get the fried chicken basket, candied yams, and collard greens," Mark said. After the waitress left, I was praying Mark didn't ask about Jax.

"So, talk to me. Tell me what your future plans are since you're not in a relationship anymore? Do you wanna ever get married?" Mark asked, and I was glad he didn't ask about Jax. I had to think about the question he just asked me. To be honest, I never thought about marriage because I was content with what me and Jax had.

"I hope to one day be someone's wife," was all I said. After I answered the question, it was a moment of silence, which seemed a little weird to me since he was the one that asked the question. I just brushed it off and started a new conversation until our food came out. I hope this ended up being a great friendship, because Lord knows I needed it.

ere it was a month later and Mark was still talking about that shit that happened at IHOP, it seemed like he was obsessed with Jaxen more and more every day. Mark must think that I'm a fool if he thought I didn't know he was back to his old ways. What he didn't know was I truly didn't care this time. The more time he spent in the streets, the more time I spent next door. Jaxen and I were doing everything you could do sexually except penetration. I knew it wouldn't be much longer before I just gave in or he just took the pussy. Jaxen had already warned me that the next time he had me alone, it was going down, and I was actually looking forward to seeing what his dick game was like. I know he could eat the hell out of some pussy.

Mark been so-called working late nights again, which I knew was a lie.

"Zoey baby, come eat!" I yelled upstairs. Zoey came downstairs, sat down at the table, and started eating right away. I made her some chicken nuggets and fries. Mark and I had plans to catch a movie and go to Friday's afterwards, so I didn't bother to make us anything. Once again Zoey was going with my parents this weekend. Mark was upstairs getting dressed so once Zoey was finished eating, we were gonna drop her off then go do our thing. Mark finally came down-stairs ready to go and after cleaning up Zoey, we headed out the door.

"I'll see you Sunday princess, mommy loves you," I told Zoey while placing a kiss on her cheeks. After saying our goodbyes, we drove off. When we got to Cherry Hill, Mark decided to stop at the mall, and I was okay with that I needed a few items from Victoria Secret.

Mark and I were walking through Cherry Hill Mall like two teenagers in love like we used to do when we first started dating. Sometimes I wished things didn't turn out the way that they did because I really used to be in love and happy with Mark. He's the only man I've ever known and wanted to know. We stopped in Macy's, and Mark grabbed some cologne, but it wasn't the fragrance that he always wore, which made me raise an eyebrow. Mark has been wearing the same cologne since high school.

"When did you change your cologne?"

"I didn't, but I want to try something new," he said. I didn't bother to respond because I knew he was full of shit. After Mark paid for his new fragrance to wear for whatever new bitch he was fucking with, we left the store and went into Victoria's Secret.

I grabbed a basket and started throwing items into the bin, but I could feel someone staring at me. When I looked up, it was the two ghetto chicks from IHOP. The pregnant girl rolled her eyes and I had just about enough of this bitch. I usually wouldn't make a scene out in the public, but I was about to make an exception for her ghetto ass. I could tell that her and the girl was talking about me, but I was really about to give them something to talk about.

"Do you have a problem with me or something? Because you seem to have a fucking eye problem ever time you see me," I snapped with an attitude.

"Baby, are you done yet? The movie will be starting soon..." Mark asked, but he paused in his tracks the moment that he saw me and the pregnant girl standing face to face.

"Baby, what's going on?" Mark asked, trying not to give the pregnant girl any eye contact, which I found a little odd. It was something about the look.

"Yeah, I'm good. Except this fucking hoodrat that keep staring at me with this other ghetto bird, so I asked her what was her problem," I told Mark.

"Mark, I suggest that you check your wife. This is the mother of your child," the other girl stated, but I just knew I heard wrong.

"Mark, what the fuck is this bitch mean, this is the mother of your child?" I snapped.

"This bitch is lying! That ain't my fucking baby! I didn't even know she was pregnant," Mark stated.

"Really, Mark? You gonna stand here deny our baby?" the pregnant girl elaborated.

"Kia, don't fucking play with me right now! You know fucking well that's not my baby!" Mark yelled, causing a scene in the store. Hearing him say her name caused my heart to drop to the pit of my stomach. Kia was the one he was cheating on me with a few months back when he was staying out all night long and for days at a time. Everything made sense now. She was the one who told him about me being at IHOP with Jaxen. My blood was boiling and Mark was about to feel my wrath. I smacked Mark so damn hard that blood flew out of his mouth.

"How dare you ruin our family with some tramp ass hoe like this?! A woman who thinks I should respect my husband's mistress? That's some funny shit! This bitch got pregnant by my husband and gon' ask me for respect!" I yelled loudly. Now I was talking to the customers that were in the store. I was sure that security was on their way to escort us out the mall. I was so pissed, and I knew I was wrong for what I did, but since I couldn't hit Kia, I punched the shit out of her mouthy friend. Because I was sick of, her shit too.

We got to rocking right there in Victoria's Secret. Mark was trying to get me off the girl but I was too far gone for that. Security finally got me off the girl and started dragging me out the store.

"Bitch, wait until you have that bastard baby of yours, I'm gonna fuck you up on sight, best believe that," I yelled before leaving out.

The guards escorted me outside and I was pissed beyond words, not to mention embarrassed. I knew my heart wasn't with Mark anymore. I've been doing things with Jaxen that I shouldn't have been doing as a married woman, but this nigga went and made a baby on me. I knew this was something that I would never be able to get past.

With tears in my eyes, I ordered a lyft. Just as my car pulled up, Mark tried to catch up to me, but he was too late. He was the last person I wanted to see, so I decided to get me a room for the night because there was no way in hell I was sleeping in the same house with Mark.

MARK

It had been two days and Zyla still hadn't returned home. I knew her parents knew where she was, but of course, they weren't telling me anything. In fact, they both had been giving me their asses to kiss. They weren't at all happy with this situation I was in. Hell, I wasn't happy with the situation I was in. I couldn't believe Kia never got rid of the baby. This chick really had me thinking that she wasn't pregnant anymore. I felt like a whole ass.

"So, what's going on in your head right now?" Josh asked, bringing me out of my thoughts.

"My thoughts are, how am I going to fix this?"

"You already know I'm about to give you the real on this situation. I don't think it's going to ever be fixed. You might as well let her go and sign them divorce papers. Because after she uses this time to clear her mind, they coming."

"Zyla is not divorcing me," I said, half smiling.

"Yeah ok...if you think so. You pushed her right into that other nigga's arms. I told you a while back you had a prize possession so treat her with the utmost respect, and you did none of that. You don't deserve her, man. Let me get out of here so I can get home to my family. Don't drink too much; you still have to drive home," Josh said and then got up and left.

I hated everything he was saying, but I knew he was right. Zyla dealt with cheating, but I knew damn well she wasn't dealing with no babies or STD's. Knowing this wasn't going to stop me from trying though.

"Bartender, give me another shot please," I said, placing another twenty on the bar. Josh and I had decided to go to happy hour at the sports bar that was close to the job. My house was only fifteen minutes away so I should have no problem with getting there.

I sat at the bar in deep thought and on my fifth shot. I was all in my feelings. Not only was I going to lose my wife, I was having a baby by a woman I knew for sure was going to drive me crazy. Kia was not mother material. She wasn't going to work, and her ass was going to be lying around, waiting for me to support her. Between her and Zyla, I was never going to have any money. Zyla has all proof of me cheating so she would get alimony, child support, and the fucking house. I was all fucked up, because I wouldn't keep my dick in my pants.

"Bartender, my glass is empty!" I yelled across the bar to get his attention. He walked over to me without a drink in his hand, so I knew he was going to be on some bullshit.

"That's it, my man. You're flagged. I either need to call you a cab, or you need to call someone to pick you up, but I can't allow you to leave out of here like this." I looked at him with the meanest mug on my face. I wasn't trying to hear none of the shit he was talking. Not wanting to stay in my house alone and not wanting to go to Kia's, I decided to call Sasha.

I dialed her number and she picked right up.

"Hello, beautiful. I know you may be busy, but will you be able to pick me up.? I'm at the Sports Bar on Chapel Ave, and the bartender said I had too much to drink to leave on my own."

"Ok. Let me slide some clothes on then I'll be right there," she said with no hesitation. When she hung up, the bartender was still standing in my damn face, getting on my damn nerves.

"Somebody is coming. Now, if you not giving me another drink, you can get the hell out of my face," I snapped, causing him to walk away. I sat there waiting with so much on my mind. The crazy part was I didn't even see this shit coming. I should have taken my ass with her to get the damn abortion instead of trusting her to go on her own.

Within twenty minutes, Sasha was walking in the bar. She had on a pair of tights, a t-shirt, and a pair of Ugg's. Even when she's dressed down, baby girl was beautiful, and her body was stacked like crazy. I tried to stand to meet her, but my ass fell right back down in the chair. I guess I was drunker than what I thought.

"Oh my god! Mark, are you okay?" She asked, running over to me.

"I'm good, baby. Just drunk as hell; I have so much shit on my mind. My wife trying to take my daughter from me and it has my feelings all over the place," I lied, trying to get her to feel just as sorry for me as I was feeling for myself.

"Everything will work out for the best. Now come on, let me get you home," Sasha said, trying to help me up out of the chair. It was a struggle, but she got me to her car and helped me get inside. I laid my head on the headrest and waited for her to get into the driver's seat.

"I don't wanna go home," I said, being truthful.

"You can come home with me; my daughter is with her god mama. I don't mind the company, plus you look like you can use someone to vent too."

———

I woke up in an unfamiliar place until I looked around and saw the pictures on the wall then I knew where I was. I went to sit up on the couch, and my head was banging. I looked at my phone and saw that it was about 2 a.m. I needed aspirin or something, so I made my way to the bathroom to look in Sasha's medicine cabinet. I didn't find anything, so I made my way to her room. To my surprise, she was sitting up with a book in her hand and some cute little reading glasses on. I stood in the door and watched her pretty ass for a couple minutes before she looked up at me, smiling.

"Hey, you. Is something wrong?" She asked.

"I have a headache and was looking for some aspirin or something."

"Oh, I'll get it for you. Come on, let's go to the kitchen," Sasha said, climbing out of her bed with these little ass boy shorts on and a crop top that read sleep. I couldn't control the way my eyes were roaming her body. Sasha knew what the hell her little ass was doing, and to be honest, she may have been what I needed to get Zyla off my mind. I followed her to the kitchen with my eyes trained and watching her ass cheeks play peekaboo. I licked my lips while shaking my head.

"I had left the aspirin in the kitchen on the table earlier. Are you hungry? Would you like something to eat?"

"No, just something to drink. Do you have any black coffee?" I asked.

"Yes, I already have the Keurig ready for my morning cup of coffee," Sasha said while walking over to the Keurig and pushing the start button. Then she sat at the table, so I decided to sit across from her.

"What are you doing up at this time? If you don't mind me asking," I asked.

"I told you some nights I tend to not get any sleep. I couldn't call you because you were already here, so I just decided to read a little."

"I saw that. I didn't know you like to read?"

"Yeah, I love too. Since I've been having a lot of time on my hands lately, I've actually been reading a whole lot. I love all types of books: romance, thrillers, and street lit. So, yup, that's one of my favorite things to do. I've even thought about writing a book," Sasha said with a smile on her face.

"Wow... I say go for it, if you got it in your mind," I said, encouraging her. The sound of the Keurig beeping bought us both out of our thoughts. Sasha jumped up, grabbed the coffee mug and handed it to me. I thanked her as she sat right back down. I knew she wanted to talk to me about why I was in the bar cutting up. So, before she asked, I was already getting my story together in my head. I knew we would probably be here talking for a minute. Hopefully, she would feel so sorry for me, I would be in her bed helping her take her skimpy ass clothes off.

It had been three days since I had been at the Holiday Inn on Route 70 and my heart was crushed. Yeah, I know Mark and I weren't on good terms, but to know he had a baby on the way with the bitch he had supposed to have stopped dealing with had me in my feelings. Not to mention, the day I left the mall, I got into a Lyft and made my way over the Jax's house, hoping he would console me. I got out of the Lyft, made my way up to his front door, but the minute I was about to knock, I looked in his window, and it was some bitch in there sucking his dick. The shit hurt me even more, but I didn't even understand why. I was still a married woman and Jax didn't have no commitment to me.

I pulled my drained body out of bed and made my way into the bathroom. Tasia was bringing Zoey to see me, so I needed to get my shit together. I didn't want my baby to see me like this, but my mama kept calling me telling me Zoey kept asking for me and Mark. I vowed that I would never let this shit get me down like this, and here I was being dumb as fuck. I always knew that nigga was doing him, so why didn't I leave him the fuck alone for my own sanity?

After I turned the water to the temperature I liked, I jumped in the shower and let the water run over my head while the tears ran down my face. This was the last time I was crying like this. I was checking out of this hotel today, and I hope Mark had somewhere to go because I wanted him out of my house. I also was meeting up with a divorce attorney today as well. It was time for me to get my shit together. I had cried over this nigga for too many years. His time was up and I needed my peace back. A half hour later, I was finished with my shower and now sitting on the bed oiling my skin so I could slide on my clothes before Tasia came. My phone vibrating on the bed next to me caught my attention. When I looked down, I saw it was a text message from Jax. I guess I was over ignoring him too.

Jaxen: I know you've been seeing me trying to get in touch with you, ma.

Me: Yes, but I've been going through some things, and I just needed some time.

Jaxen: This ain't what we do, Zyla. I thought we were better than this.

Me: I thought we were too until I saw baby girl sucking ya dick.

I hit send, but I wish that didn't. I knew I had no right getting mad at him for doing him, but I just couldn't seem to get that shit off my mind. It was like both the men that were in my life betrayed me. It took him a minute to respond, but I knew he would.

Jaxen: Sorry for you seeing that, ma, but that still is no reason for you not to reach out. Where you at? How are you? Do you need anything?"

Me: I'm good, Jax. Like I said I just needed some time to myself.

Jaxen: Ok...well, your time is up now. When can I see you? And don't play with me, Zyla. I will hire a private detective to find ya little ass. I was about to knock on your door a couple of times, but I decided against it. I didn't wanna have to kill your baby daddy for acting tough.

Me: You don't have to do all that, Jax. As soon as I get finished handling my business today, I'll text you.
Jaxen: I'll be waiting.

It was no need to respond to him because I knew how he was serious, and if I took forever to see him, he would do exactly what he said. I slipped my clothes on and made my way to the seating area of the hotel room to wait for my best friend. As soon as I was about to sit down, there was a knock at the door. When I opened it, all that was standing there was Tasia. I looked at her with a sad look on my face.

"Where is Zoey at?"

"Aht Aht, don't look at me with that sad ass face. I wasn't bringing her; she would have asked you a million questions. We are going to get her and go to dinner or something. You know damn well you don't want her asking questions about you being in no damn hotel, so don't start," Tasia said, brushing past me.

Tasia had a point. I swear she was my best friend for a reason. I just wished I would have listened to her when we were younger, and she told me Mark wasn't shit. Even though I paid her no damn mind and married his sorry ass, she still didn't turn her back on me. She may have distanced herself a little, but whenever I called, she showed up with a shoulder to cry on.

"Why didn't I listen to you, when you tried to tell me? I put this all on myself."

"Nope, don't start ya shit. You dealt with it, you hurt, you cried. Now it's time to cut all that sulking shit out and get back to normal. Ain't no blaming yourself for no fuckboy's actions. Now get ya stuff; we getting the fuck out of this damn room," Tasia said, causing me to shake my head. Sometimes she pisses me off, but the bluntness be exactly what I need for me to get my shit in order.

After I grabbed my things, we made our way to the front desk so I could check out. Then we went to get in her car. Before she started the car up, she turned her music on and of course had it blasting. *Beyoncé's Irreplaceable* blared through the car as we peeled off.

To the left, to the left.

Everything you own in the box to the left
In the closet that's my stuff, yes...

I sat and watched my bff as she sang and danced in her seat while she drove. The shit had me cracking up because I knew exactly what she was doing. It was definitely working, so I joined her and we yelled the lyrics until the song finished. Once it was off, she turned the music off and looked at me with a huge smile on her face.

"Why you looking at me like that?" I asked.

"Because you're too beautiful to let this get to you. I'm going to help you get over this in every way I can. Even if that means you have to come live with me for a while, and stop not answering Jax. He has nothing to do with Mark being a bitch made nigga. Jax likes you a lot, but you can't expect him to put his life on hold while you still parade around town with your husband. Yeah, I know what happened because Khi told me. Me and him have been kicking it since breakfast."

Hearing her say that told me that Jax must have told his boy that I was mad because I caught him getting his dick sucked. I knew I didn't have a right to get mad, but shit, I was already in my damn feelings. I didn't say anything to Tasia, I just laid my head back on the headrest in deep thought. I did miss Jax with everything in me. We weren't supposed to be, but we had already developed some type of relationship, whether it was a friendship or something more.

It was two days after I had text Zyla and she still hadn't reached out. Today I was going to get me a private investigator until Khi called me with the address to Tasia's crib where Zyla was. I had pulled up in front of her house ten minutes ago, trying to figure out how I was going to approach Zyla. I knew about everything that went down and I felt bad for her. I knew she didn't love Mark anymore, but I also knew this shit hurt her bad as fuck. All she always was worried about was Zoey having both of her parents. I hopped out of the car and walked up the front steps. I knew she was there alone, so I hoped she opened the door. I knocked on the door five times before Zyla finally opened it. When she opened it, her hair was all over her head, and she was wiping the sleep out of her eyes. I could tell she wasn't expecting to see me standing here.

"Jax...what are you doing here?" She asked while trying to close her robe all the way.

"I needed to see how my baby was doing. You good?" I asked.

Zyla walked into my arms, wrapping her arms around my neck, hugging me tight. I knew she was crying, so I didn't do anything but continue to hold her until she pulled away.

"Jaxen, I'm so sorry. I've just been going through so much shit.

I've missed you so much, but after finding out about the baby and then seeing you in your living room, my feelings were just all over the place," she said just above a whisper. I pulled her back so she could look at me. I then wiped the tears from her eyes and kissed her cheek.

"You don't have to be sorry, ma. Shit happens, but we gone get over this, okay? Now come on and let's get in this house so we can talk some more."

"I don't wanna talk, Jax. I just want you to make me feel better. I just want you to take my mind off everything that's going on right now," Zyla said seductively while grabbing my hand and leading the way.

Once we made it to the room, Zyla pulled me on to the bed and started taking my clothes off. I wanted to stop her because I knew she was still in her feelings, but at the same time, I had been waiting for this for such a long time. Zyla released me from my pants in a fast motion, not missing a beat. She then looked into my eyes sexily while she placed her soft lips on mine. After she released my dick, she pointed it at her center. I entered her nice and slow, feeling her sweet spot gripping me from every angle.

"Fuck, Zyla! This pussy feels so fucking good," I groaned as I entered her. It seemed like I had been waiting for forever to be inside her and feel her, but it was worth every second that I had to wait. Zyla was squirming and digging a hole in my back as I begin to slowly stroke in and out of her tightness.

"Oh god, Jaxen, you feel so good," Zyla cooed in my ear, making my dick brick up even more. I sped up my strokes as I felt myself on the verge of cumming.

"Fuck! You about to make me cumm'," I groaned.

"Oh god, Jaxen! I'm cumming!" Zyla moaned in the sexiest tone I've ever heard. After we both came together, I stared Zyla in the eyes before gently kissing her lips. Zyla had a nigga sprung. It took everything in me not to tell her that I loved her, but when she had disappeared for those couple of days, that's when I realized it.

All the time that Zyla and I had been spending together, our feelings for each other had grown stronger. The only thing that was in our way was that sucka ass nigga of a husband she had. I'm not even going to lie; I was happy about her finding out about the baby. That way she could leave his simple ass alone. I was upset she was hurting, but I was going to be right by her side to pick up the pieces. Zyla deserved the world and so much more, and I knew that I could be the one to give it to her. I knew I did my shit with women from time to time, but the minute Zyla and I made shit official, I was done with all them chicks. What really took the cake with this fuck nigga was him still fucking with the same chick he been dealing with for years and had the nerve to get her pregnant. Then when she told me the name, I put two and two together and realized it was the same chick Khi was fucking with. This was a small world. That explained how he knew we were at Ihop together.

"Baby, you good?" I asked Zyla because she looked like she was in deep thought about some shit.

"Yes, I'm great. Thanks to you," Zyla flirted.

"You better stop flirting with me like that before I put this dick back in you," I told her seriously.

"Well, in that case, I think I'll keep on flirting," Zyla stated, climbing on top of me. The first round went so fast that I didn't mind getting a second one started. Zyla and I spent the rest of the night fucking and sucking every inch of one another's body as if we had no care in the world.

My phone ringing over and over again woke me up out of my sleep, I looked at the clock on the nightstand and it read 2:30 a.m. I found my phone, and it was an unknown number, so I answered immediately.

"Hello, may I speak to Jaxen please?"

"Speaking. Who's this?' I asked.

"This is Nurse Katlin from Cooper Hospital. Your grandma was brought in and you're listed as her emergency contact. We need you to come to the hospital."

"What the hell is wrong with my grandma? Is she okay?" I asked, panicking.

"I'm sorry, but we can't discuss her medical state over the phone," the nurse stated. I banged on her ass and started getting dressed.

"Jaxen, what's going on?" Zyla asked.

"That was a nurse from Cooper Hospital; something is wrong with my G-mom, so I gotta go," I told her while putting on my clothes.

"I'm coming with you," Zyla replied, getting up and putting her clothes on. I didn't object because I could really use the company and support. As soon as we were dressed, we shot out the door. On the way to the hospital. I shot Khi a text telling him to meet me at the hospital. I pulled up to the hospital in ten minutes, and when I walked in, I went straight to the reception desk.

"I'm here for my grandma, Pamela Taylor."

"Okay, let me call the doctor for you," the chick said with googly eyes and a flirtatious tone. I just shook my head because these chicks were so thirsty these days. A few minutes later, the doctor came out and walked over to me and Zyla.

"Hi, I'm Doctor Dorsey. Your grandmother suffered from a mild heart attack, but she appears to be doing pretty well. We just have a few more tests to run, and if everything checks out good, then she should be free to go home in a couple of days. We're trying to get her blood pressure down because when she was brought in, it was a little elevated. Your grandmother is lucky that someone was there with her at the time or else this may have not turned out too good," the doctor stated. I heard everything that the doctor said, but all I wanted to know was who the hell was at the house with her at this hour.

"You can go to see her when you're ready." Zyla and I headed to the back and as I got closer to the room, I could hear my grandmother's voice talking. When I walked in the room, I was confused about who the hell the man was that was at my grandma's bedside.

"Hey, G-mom. Are you okay?" I asked.

"Yeah, I'm good. Just wish I could go home because all they gonna do is poke and prod all night long."

"What happened?" I asked.

"I started having a little chest pain, but I thought it was heartburn until I felt a sharp pain shoot through my chest and I felt like I couldn't breathe. I told John to call the ambulance and I'm glad that he was there, otherwise I may have died."

"I'm glad that you're okay, but who the hell is John?"

"This is John, he's a close friend of mine, and John, this is my grandson Jaxen. Apparently, he thinks he's my daddy," my G-mom stated. "And speaking of friends, who's this lovely lady that you have here with you at this hour?" My grandma asked.

"I'm sorry. This is my very close friend, Zyla, and Zyla, this is my grandma Pam," I introduced my two favorite ladies.

"Hi. I'm sorry we had to meet like this, but it's nice to meet you, and I'm really glad that you're okay," Zyla said.

"Thank you, sweetie. You seem like a nice lady; I'll have to have you over for dinner soon." Khi walked in the room and looked surprised to see Zyla and the mystery dude, but he didn't say anything. We sat in the room for a little while longer before heading out. I was glad that my G-mom was okay because I don't know what the hell I would do if something was to happen to her.

When I woke up the next day, I looked at the clock. It was the afternoon and I was still tired as shit. I looked over and Zyla wasn't in bed, but there was a note on the pillow letting me know that she left for class. I got up and made my way home so I can shower then head to the hospital to check on my G-mom. When I got there, her and Khi was talking so I stood in the doorway and listened for a few moments before making my presence known.

"So, what do you know about that Zyla girl that Jax had with him last night?"

"All I know is she's his neighbor and he's super in love with her. They spend a lot of time together and I'm dating her best friend."

"Tell me that's not the married woman he was talking about a few months back?

"Yeah, that's her, G-mom. And like Khi has already told you, I'm in love with her. But enough about Zyla, who the hell was that nigga John, and how come I haven't heard about him until now?"

"John is my old man, if you must know. We've been dating for about three months and I didn't tell you about him because we just got serious, we were just fucking at first," my grandma sassed, almost making me puke.

"Come on, grandma, don't nobody wanna hear that shit. That's just nasty," I stated, mad as hell. Khi was laughing his ass off, but I didn't see shit funny. Before I could respond to the fuckery, the doctor walked in.

"Good afternoon, Ms. Taylor. All of your test results came back good, so it doesn't look like you have to stay any more days. You can go home as soon as the nurse comes in with your paperwork. Just make sure to follow up with your primary doctor," the doctor stated. After seeing if we had any questions, he left the room.

———

LATER THAT EVENING, I WENT HOME AND GOT MY GUEST ROOM together for my G-mom. She finally agreed to come stay with me for a few weeks so she wouldn't be home alone. Tonight, she decided to go to that nigga John's house. I wasn't feeling that shit but what could I do to stop them? I mean, I could always kill his ass but then my grandma's heart would be broken. All I could think about was Zyla's sexy ass. I knew she wouldn't be ready to make shit official, but I was about to take care of every part of her. I never thought I'd see the day when a nigga like me would fall in love with a married chick and I wasn't even getting no pussy. Once I was done with my grandma's room, I went downstairs to pour myself a drink, but my doorbell rang before I had the chance to pour it. I went to the door and it was Khi and this nigga was smiling from ear to ear.

"You ready to go handle this business? Or you just gone stand there with that big Kool aide smile on your face? What the fuck you smiling so hard for?" I inquired.

"I think I'm in love," that nigga stated.

"Nigga, shut your stupid ass up, When the hell does Khi Parker fall in love?"

"The day a nigga like me just had the best dick suck there is to have," Khi replied, causing me to bust out in laughter.

"I swear your ass should have been a damn comedian with the stupid shit that comes out of your mouth. Did you handle the shit with Cliff in them?" I asked. See I was easing my way off the streets which is why Khi handled all of that. I was basically the nigga behind the scenes. The street shit was temporary for me and as soon as I got my house and the woman, I was ready to settle down with. I knew I was about to stray away.

"Yes...I handled all of that. I even assigned them all to new traps. Next week when I collect, I'll let you know how everything is working. But I'm serious as hell right now about baby girl. I'm thinking about asking her to make this shit official," Khi said seriously. I looked at my bro and could see that he was dead ass.

"That's what's up, bro. I'm glad you found someone that makes you happy. Do you think this shit is going to mess up what we got going on business wise?" I asked.

Nah...she knows what I do, and we talked about all of that. I know how to handle my street shit and my personal life. Plus, I'ma be the head nigga in charge soon, right? So, I got this now let me do me." Khi just gave me a head nod and poured himself a drink.

"Alright bro...I was just making sure. You know how we get when that LOVE word gets involved, but you already know. I don't mind coming out of retirement to help you with anything. I'ma still be the back man for a minute until you get right." I assured Khi.

"I know man...you got me just like I got you. Now, what's going on with you and your craziness?" Khi asked while drinking from his drink he just poured.

"Honestly, shit is going all right so far. Me and Zyla been fucking like two teenagers in love. I know I'm being selfish, but I wanted her to be completely done with her husband and all the feelings that she has for him, so I can have her to myself. I mean, she filed for a divorce, but that's a process."

"Yeah, I feel you. If that's meant to be your girl, then she will be. On another note, where the hell is your crazy ass baby mama?" Khi asked.

"Hell, if you wanna know the truth, she's been staying out of my hair. She doesn't call or text me at all unless it's about Jayla and those convo's be short as shit," I replied.

"Another nigga must be hitting that because there's no way in hell that crazy ass girl just left you alone out of the blue."

I thought about what Khi said and that nigga was probably right. Oh well, that was their problem now.

This shit with Mark has been so overwhelming and stressful. Knowing that one day in the near future I may have to explain to Zoey that she has a sibling, one that has a different mother, is all I could think about. How could Mark be so selfish and do this to our family and get another woman pregnant? I was so lucky to have Jax and Tasia to help me get through all of this. Although I sometimes feel like shit is moving too fast with me and Jax, I had to admit that I was really feeling him, and he was a great distraction. I could honestly say that I was having the best sex of my life. Jax knew how to eat pussy and he damn sure knew how to lay pipe. Mark and I have been together so many years; he had been my first and only man, so I never had anyone to compare Mark too.

I was on my way to my parent's house to see what the hell my mother wanted. I was almost sure that she was gonna piss me off per usual, but I couldn't stay long because I was meeting with Mark and our lawyers soon. When I walked into my parent's house, I could smell the aroma of food and coffee in the air. My dad was sitting in the living room, which meant I could find my mother in the kitchen.

"Hey, daddy," I spoke, planting a kiss on my dad's cheek.

"Hey, princess. How are you feeling?" My dad asked.

"Some days are better than others, but I'm coming along okay. I'm just hurt, but I'll get through it," I told my dad honestly.

"Yes, you will, princess. It's his loss, not yours. You say the word and I'll body his ass if you want me to. The only reason that nigga is still breathing is because of Zoey," my dad stated. I knew my dad was serious because he didn't play about me. My father was the total opposite of my mother and I spent most of my life trying to figure out what my dad saw in her. Don't get me wrong, my mother was beautiful, smart and could dress her ass off but she was the most annoying, stuck-up woman I knew. My dad, on the other hand, was more hood and down to earth.

"I know you would, daddy, but he's not worth it. He'll get what's coming to him, trust me. Let me get in this kitchen and see what your wife wants. I'm meeting with Mark and our lawyers when I leave here." Before I could make it to the kitchen, my mother walked into the living room.

"I thought I heard you come in. Well, I came to tell both of you that breakfast was ready."

"Hey, momma," I spoke as me and my dad got up to head to the kitchen.

"Hello, Zyla," my mom replied with a half-smile. My dad and I went to the kitchen and took our seats. Halfway through my meal, my mother opened her mouth, and I knew it wouldn't have been long before I was telling her off and storming out.

"How's Zoey doing with everything that has been going on?"

"She seems to be okay for now, as far as I know. I plan to sit her down and really explain to her what's going on and how things are going to be moving forward," I answered.

"Zyla, I know everything that's happening with you and Mark right now is heartbreaking, but are you sure that a divorce is what you really want to do?" My mom asked, causing me to look up at her with disgust written all over my face. There was no way in hell that she was for real.

"Mom, I know you're not serious? Please tell me that you're not suggesting that I stay with a man that cheated on me and got one of his side chicks pregnant?" I yelled.

"Zyla, calm down and watch your tone. What the hell did you think marriage was about? Did you think that you would never be cheated on and just live a happy life without any problems? Marriage takes hard work. You took vows, Zyla," my mother stated, pissing me off. I could literally feel my blood boiling.

"You know what, mom? I knew you were fucked up in the head, but I didn't know you were that fucked up. What kind of mother tells her only daughter to stay with a man that not only broke his vows but cheated and got another woman pregnant? You always did think so highly of Mark, so if you like him that much then you fucking marry him!" I yelled, getting up from the table.

"Dad, I'm so sorry and mom, lose my number until you come to your senses and you're ready to be a mother," I snapped before storming out. I had never spoken to my mother like that before but she deserved it.

I jumped in my car and headed to my meeting. My mother was crazy as hell for even suggesting some stupid shit like that. Sometimes. some of the things my mom said made me wonder what type of man my father really is or was, cause she be speaking like she has experienced this type of shit before. When I walked in the lawyer's office, everyone was already there. As soon as I sat down, my lawyer didn't waste any time getting to the point.

"My client is asking for half of everything, plus alimony and child support for their daughter. Oh yeah and the house," my lawyer stated. I didn't say a word because there was nothing to say. I wanted what I wanted and I was gonna get it. Mark whispered something to his lawyer then the lawyer said something back to him before speaking.

"My client doesn't have any objections to what your client is asking for, besides the child support. My client doesn't feel like he should have to pay child support for his daughter since he has always taken care of her and will continue to do so. My client is also asking for joint custody and visitation rights. He would like the two of them to split the holidays, and he wants to be able to be a part of and attend any birthday parties that your client will have for their daughter," Mark's lawyer stated. My lawyer leaned over in my ear to ask what were my thoughts.

"My client has no objections to your client's request," my lawyer replied. The truth was even though I was pissed and hurt by Mark, I knew that he would always take care of Zoey. Zoey was Mark's pride and joy.

"May I please speak freely?" Mark asked. My lawyer looked over at me and I nodded my head in approval.

"Zyla, I just wanted to tell you that I'm truly sorry for all the hurt and pain that I've caused you. I know that my actions may not show it, but you truly are the love of my life, and there will never be another you no matter who I date in the future. I planned to come in here today and beg to save my marriage with you, but then I realized that I should just let you go. I know deep down I'm not worthy of a woman like you. Zyla, you deserve the best and you deserve to be someone's one and only," he expressed.

"I know that I probably couldn't give you that no time soon. And I've already been selfish enough to ask for you to stick around until I get it right. And as far as the Kia situation, I'm sorry but I do want to tell you this, I had no idea that she was pregnant. She did tell me that she was pregnant, but I gave her money to have an abortion and she said she did. I honestly haven't seen her or talked to her. I broke it off with her but that's no excuse because if I wasn't cheating in the first place, none of this would have happened. I don't want to be enemies, Zyla. We have a daughter and I don't want her to be in the middle of our mess that I created. I love you and I always will," Mark said sincerely with tears in his eyes. For a moment I wanted to call off my divorce and see if we could work it out, but I knew that wasn't possible. My eyes were filled with tears as different waves of emotions hit me.

"Mark, thank you for the good times. I don't want to be your enemy, but I also don't want to be your wife anymore either. I don't know if we'll ever be friends, but we can be cordial," was all I said. After signing some paperwork, the meeting was over, and I walked away from my childhood sweetheart. I walked away from the man that I thought I would spend the rest of my life with. Although it hurt like hell to walk away, I finally felt free.

Mark had me all the way fucked up if he thought that he was going to ignore me and leave me to deal with this baby by myself. I know that I told him I had an abortion, but now that he knows that I didn't, he still wasn't fucking with me. I knew that him and his precious wife was no longer together, and the fact that I still haven't seen or talked to him let me know that he must have been fucking someone else, so I decided to play detective, and I was right. I had been following Mark around for the last few weeks and he was spending a lot of time with some bitch named Sasha. I just couldn't let that be. He was about to get this bitch fucked up if he thought he was just gonna move on.

Mark had gotten an apartment not too far from where he used to live with his now ex-wife. I don't know what my obsession was with Mark, but that nigga had me gone. I mean, I've had issues with men like him, so this wasn't new. I had chances of being with single men, but married men were just my type. I think what made Mark different was he finally was going to make me a mommy. I've had a couple of miscarriages in the past, but this pregnancy was going well —which meant that Mark and I had something special.

This pregnancy had my hormones all over the place. The shit had me thinking all kinds of crazy shit. Which made me come to the conclusion that Mark and his new bitch may not be safe around me at all. I'm definitely a little off and I'm gonna get what the fuck I want, or things may start happening that I have no control over. The fact that it seemed like he was really feeling Sasha, angered me something terrible. I had found out her name by doing some research. When I found out she was the baby mama of Jaxen that made this even more interesting. Right then and there, I knew I had to be on my shit.

Jax was not a nigga to piss off, so I was going to do a little more research then go from there. If you ever lived in the hood you heard about Jaxen Taylor, if you didn't you were basically a nobody. I did find out that he wasn't in the streets like he use to be. Since Khi took over, see Khi was some dude I use to fuck from time to time. He was good to keep my mind off of Mark, but then when Mark was back in the picture, I gave Khi my ass to kiss. This was another reason why I was pissed off. I practically gave my heart to Mark. I let his ass know he was the only one and he still don't give a fuck. I knew one thing for sure, I would have to put a stop to this. If I couldn't have Mark Holmes, then no one would.

"Girl, what you in here doing?" My sister, Kesha, asked, walking into my room.

"Nothing, just sitting here thinking about Mark. I need to find out if he wants an invitation to the baby shower." Kesha looked at me with a raised brow.

"Kia... Mark doesn't want you, so I wish you leave that man alone. You've did enough. You already messed up that man's marriage. I'm not sure what happened to you over the years, but you really get a kick out of being involved with someone else's man. Why?" Kesha asked with an attitude.

My sister got on my fucking nerves. I knew her ass was just mad because she recently just went through a divorce. Shit, that wasn't my fucking problem. Ain't nobody told her to marry Joe's broke cheating ass. She already knew he was cheating before she married him. Now she hates every woman that messes with men that are involved with someone. If they were happy at home, they wouldn't give me the time of day. So, I do what I do and give them what they want. I am the calm after the storm. Don't no man wanna get off work and go home to a nagging ass chick. If Kesha would have just let that man cheat in peace, her dumb ass would still be married, but nope, she walking around here unhappy, thinking that she'll never be loved again. These chicks be real crazy. Shit, when and if I ever get married, I want that shit to be open. As long as the other woman not getting more attention than me, we should be good. Our relationship will always be straight.

"Kesha, don't start your shit, because I'm not in the mood. Why don't you just call Joe? I'm sure he will take your depressed ass back with no problem," I sassed, grabbing my purse and keys and then walked out. It was time for me to spy on Mark.

Once I made it out of the house, I jumped in my truck, threw my shades on and put some music on. After I placed my seatbelt on, I peeled off on my way to Mark's job hoping I could get Sasha's address. If I had to stalk his ass all week to find out what I needed to find out, then I would do so. I needed to get ready for the birth of this baby soon, and I refused not to have Mark by my side when I give birth.

———

THE WHOLE TIME I SAT OUTSIDE MARK'S JOB, I CALLED HIS phone back to back, and he didn't answer. I found that real fucked up when I saw him look at his phone and put it in his pocket. Then right before he got in his car, his phone rung again, and he picked right up. The shit pissed me right the fuck off, causing me to punch the staring wheel. When he jumped in his car and peeled off, I followed right behind him. A half hour later, we were pulling up to a cute little townhouse. I didn't know whose home it was, but it had a nice, cute little Lexus truck sitting in the driveway.

I watched Mark walk up the two steps that lead to the front door, and watched it fly open. What I saw caused my blood to boil. Sasha opened the door in a silk purple robe and pulled Mark in for a passionate kiss. She then pulled him in the house and closed the door. I was frustrated, but I knew I had to go on with my plan. I couldn't just blow off the handle right now. I was going to play my cards right. I wanted to push her away from Mark, that way he would come running back to me and his unborn child.

After sitting there for another fifteen minutes trying to get my thoughts in order, I rambled through my purse and found my hot pink lipstick. Then I grabbed a piece of paper out of my glove compartment and decided to leave little Ms. Sasha a note on her car.

I wrote big as hell: YOU'RE NOT THE ONLY ONE! Then I put some lipstick on my lips then puckered up and kissed the note. Once I placed the note on her car, I got in mine and peeled off. I was tired and this baby was doing a lot of damn movement.

I made it back to my house with so much shit on my mind. I hoped to God that Kesha left and went somewhere else because I wasn't trying to hear much more of her shit. I wish her and her husband got it together because I would ship her and her belongings right there. I was sick of her being here with me, but no matter how much she got on my nerves, I was my sister's keeper. We may have not gotten along, but we always had each other's back.

Once I got to my bedroom, I stripped out of my clothes and looked in the mirror at my protruding belly. I couldn't believe that I was just about six months. The time went by fast as hell. Not too long ago I was sitting out at the abortion clinic. While sitting there, a lot came to mind about me miscarrying and I just couldn't go with killing the baby. Not when there was hope for me to finally be a mother. Now here I was getting ready for my little pumpkin, who will be arriving soon. I looked at myself one more time in the mirror before I headed into the bathroom to take my shower. I had to wash this crazy day I had off me. Not to mention, my feet were hurting and my body was tired.

MARK

I had a great night with Sasha, even though I was still fucked up about the situation with me and Zyla. I didn't mean her no good though. She had put up with my bullshit for many years, but with the baby on the way, I know I crushed the shit out of her. Even though I knew she wasn't in love with me anymore. Hell, I crushed the shit out of myself the first time Kia told me she was pregnant. All the years I had been cheating on Zyla, none of the women ever popped up pregnant. So, yeah, I was getting comfortable with all the bullshit I was doing.

"You good, baby?" Sasha asked, sashaying into the room.

She was beautiful and was definitely taking my mind off all the bullshit I was going through. I was taking the day off today because I was going to pick Zoey up so we can go out. Until then, I was hoping I could chill with Sasha's beautiful ass.

"Yes, I'm good. Thanks to the amazing night you gave me, beautiful. What's on your agenda today?"

"Well, nothing til' later. Jayla and I are supposed to have a mother-daughter day. I would ask you to come along, but I know that would be too soon to be asking you to bring her around me."

"I don't see anything wrong with us having a play date for the girls. There's really nothing my ex can say. She does what she does during her time with my daughter and I do what I want when it's my turn. So, I would love that. Now come over here and let's continue from last night, then we can go out to breakfast or some- thing." I beamed, signaling Sasha over to me.

"I don't wanna go out to breakfast. I wanna cook you breakfast after we continue from last night," Sasha cooed, straddling me.

Once Sasha climbed on top of me, I pulled her robe open and plopped one of her perky titties in my mouth, causing her to lean her head back and let out a soft moan. The sounds of her moans caused me to brick right up. Sasha and I were about to explore each other a little more.

———

I HAD ALREADY GOTTEN ZOEY AND WE WERE WALKING INTO THE Deptford Mall to meet up with Jayla and Sasha. I had to have a little talk with Zoey before we went in, because I didn't want her to feel any type of way.

"Baby, we are meeting a friend of mine and her daughter Jayla. We figured since y'all were around the same age that y'all could have a playdate. Is that okay with you?"

"Yesss, daddy. I love playdates and she's got the same name as my new friend that mommy let me meet," Zoey cooed in excitement.

I looked at my baby and smiled at how excited she was to meet a new friend. Nothing else was said. Since my baby was comfortable with it, I was happy. So, we made our way into the mall and straight to the food court to meet up with Sasha. I had shot her a text a little while ago and she said they would be near Chick Fil-a in the food court.

We made it to the food court, but I didn't see Sasha anywhere. I stood for a second until I heard a little girl's voice calling Zoey. I turned around towards where the voice was coming from and saw Sasha standing there facing me. As soon as Zoey saw Jayla, she went running over to her, and they both hugged each other. Sasha and I both stood in shock.

"Mommy, this is my new friend Zoey, she lives next door from daddy." Hearing lil' mama say that caused my eyes to get big. Now that I heard her say that, it explains why the day Sasha mentioned the name Jax, she got quiet after a while. All this time, I had been kicking with the nigga that stole my wife away from my baby mama. This shit was weird as hell. Now I was sitting here wondering how long Zyla been having that hood ass dude around my fucking daughter for our kids to be so damn friendly.

"So, you're the neighbor's husband, huh?" Sasha asked.

I chuckled, while shaking my head. "This shit is a crazy coincidence. If you wanna call this quits right now before we even get started, we can," I said.

"No, we good. We're just two single people enjoying each other's company. So, come on. Let's go have fun with these girls before they start complaining."

"Alright cool. Let me go use the bathroom real quick then we can go," I assured Sasha while making my way over to the other side to use the men's room. A part of me wanted to let this shit go, but another part of me just couldn't. I walked into the bathroom, pulled my phone out and dialed Zyla's number. The phone rung about four times before she decided to pick up.

"How long you been bringing my daughter around this thug, Zyla?"

"Mark, what the fuck are you talking about?"

"Zyla, I swear to God if something happens to my daughter while you with that nigga, you'll never get to see her again because I'll make sure of it."

"Mark, I don't know what the fuck you're talking about, but we're divorced, and I could have my daughter around anybody I want. What you think, I'm just gone stay single while your out here doing you?"

"I don't give a fuck what you do, Zyla, but I don't want my daughter around no damn drug dealers."

"Mark, FUCK YOU!" Zyla said, hanging up in my ear. I looked at my phone in disbelief. I guess being around that dude was making her change. Zyla has never talked to me the way she has for the past six months, and this shit was getting way out of control. I wanted us to be more cordial, but it was like the shit wasn't working. Before I left the bathroom, I got my anger under control. I couldn't let Sasha and the girls see me like this. Especially Zoey, she was already having a hard time dealing with me and her mama's breakup. So I was going to do whatever in my power to make sure she continues to live the happy life she's been living. I never want her to feel any different because of what Zyla and I are going through. I got my shit together and walked out of the bathroom. Sasha and the girls were sitting there waiting for me. When Zoey finally saw me, she jumped up and ran my way.

"Daddy, you took long. I wanna go to Justice to get more clothes... please," Zoey said, smiling at me.

"Sorry daddy took long and we can go wherever you want, baby. Come on, you and Jayla could pick out three outfits a piece. If that's ok with Jayla's mommy."

"Yeah, it's cool. Come on, girls. Let's go," Sasha said and both the girls grabbed her hand. I still had me and Zyla's conversation in my head, but I wasn't going to let it ruin my night.

"What's the matter, baby? What you in here hollering about?" Jax asked, walking back in his bedroom. Jax and I had been kicking it real heavy since my divorce. It's been a couple months and we just couldn't get enough of each other. Mark and I had been arguing like crazy because he didn't want Zoey around Jax, but it was okay for her to be around Sasha. Mark had a lot of fucking nerve, and y'all heard me right— Sasha. Mark and her had been dealing with each other since the divorce and the shit was so awkward.

"Mark, back on his bullshit, but it's nothing to be alarmed about. I can handle it, baby," I said, pulling Jax in for a hug.

"I told you say the word and I'll beat his bitch ass up. I've been chillin' for the sake of you and Zoey, but if he keeps his shit up, I'ma step to his ass and I mean it, Zyla."

I knew Jax was being good worried about our feelings, but I also knew I wasn't going to be able to hold him down too much longer. I just don't know why the fuck Mark won't let me be happy. He moved on so why I can't.

"I know, baby. I know and please let me handle it," I said while

. . .

RUNNING MY HAND DOWN HIS TATTED CHEST. THE LOOK HE GAVE me while I rubbed his chest turned me on, so I leaned in to kiss his lips. I knew I was starting something, but I didn't mind because I knew I was going to finish it.

Jaxen dropped his ballers, causing me to bite down on my bottom lip. I stared, watching his erection grow longer right before my eyes. I dropped on the bed waiting impatiently for Jax to enter me. Once his lips touched mine, I closed my eyes, feeling his erec- tion enter me slowly. As he moved in and out of me in a slow motion, my eyes rolled in the back of my head, enjoying Jax hitting every spot.

"Damn, ma," he groaned, while continuing to penetrate me, taking my breath away. "Shit feels good. Don't it, ma?"

"Yess...baby, so damn good," I moaned out in pleasure, while Jax continued to do beautiful things to my body.

Jax was hitting every spot, even ones that I didn't even know I had. The shit was feeling so good I decided to just bask in my glory and let him take my body to another place. Jax looked down at me and I just couldn't help myself. I wrapped my arms around his neck, pulled him in and kissed him vigorously. I was grinding my hips, trying to meet him stroke for stroke. The way we both were moaning let me know that we both were ready to climax.

"Please, Jax! Don't stop, baby! Don't stop!" I yelled out in his ear as my body started to shake. I knew right then and there that I was cummin' and Jax came right behind me. Jax fell on the side of me and we both were out of breath. Once we got our shit together, he leaned in to kiss my forehead.

"I like how ya pretty ass changed the subject, but I'm serious, Zyla. If he keeps it up, I'ma fuck him up, and I mean it," Jax said, causing me to shake my head. I couldn't really say shit. I knew how he felt about me being disrespected and Mark was going overboard with the dumb shit. It's like every time I turned around, he had a

PROBLEM WITH SOMETHING. I DIDN'T SAY ANYTHING TO JAX

about how he felt. I just kissed his lips and pulled him closer to me so we could take a nap.

———

THE SOUND OF HARD BANGING ON MY FRONT DOOR WOKE ME and Jax from our nap. I looked up and Jax was already throwing something on to go open the door, so I rolled back over to go back to sleep. Jax came back a couple minutes later with his face all torn up.

"Babe, go get ya mama before I put her ignorant ass out my house. I'm being respectful because I was taught that way, but she ain't gone come to my house talking shit and I ain't did shit to her."

I didn't even say shit. I just got up and grabbed my robe and put it on. I couldn't believe her ass came over here and knocked on his door. I know nobody, but Mark's ass told her I'm over here. I was starting to get annoyed because every time I turned around, it was always some bullshit going on. Once I made it downstairs, she was standing there looking at me all crazy.

"Mama, what the hell are you doing here?"

"Zyla, I should be asking you the same thing. I heard this man is a drug dealer and here my one and only daughter is parading around town with this man. I don't like this at all. You should have just stayed with your husband, but you rather be with a drug dealer."

"Mama, lower your damn voice before he hears you. And I don't know why you keep asking about me staying with my cheating ass husband. This man made a fucking baby on me and you think I was supposed to stay with him. Girl, you crazy as hell." I hated talking to my mama like this, but she was straight tripping.

SHE STOOD THERE WITH HER HAND OVER HER MOUTH LIKE SHE was shocked at what I said.

"Oh yeah, you showing out. Messing with this man got you

talking to me all crazy. I can't believe this, Zyla. I'm your mother and you need to have a little more respect."

"Mama, you practice what you preach. Now, if you would excuse me, I would love to go lay back under my man and maybe you should do the same," I said while walking her to the front door. My mama sucked her teeth then stormed out the front door.

"Zyla, you better make sure my granddaughter stays safe since this is the trash you wanna deal with," she sassed while she got into her car. I locked the door then made my way back upstairs. Jax was lying on the bed looking up at the ceiling.

"I'm sorry about this. I'm sorry that I come with all this bullshit and this past couple of months have been a transition for you."

"I'm good, baby girl. I knew you came with some baggage. That don't take away from how I feel about you. I don't care what anybody thinks of me. I know what I do, but I'm working on getting out of it, and we talked about this already. So, who gives a fuck what any of them think? Don't beat yourself up thinking about it. I'm not stressed, because I wanted you. Now that I got you, I'ma do everything in my power to keep you and lil' Ms. Zoey happy," Jax assured me.

I straddled him, kissed his lips then laid my head on his chest. I was still tired, thanks to my mama waking us up.

"I know we just started out, Jax, but I think I'm falling in love with you."

"I been falling for you, baby girl," Jax said, kissing my forehead.

This was all new to me, but the heart wants what the heart wants and here I was confessing my love to a hustler.

———

LATER THAT NIGHT, JAX AND I WERE LAID UP WATCHING MOVIES on Netflix. I didn't have to worry about leaving him because Zoey was with Mark for the weekend. My cell ringing broke me from my thoughts. I grabbed my phone and it was my father calling, so I didn't bother to answer. I figured my mom had told him about how I spoke to her earlier, and I didn't want to listen to his shit tonight. I swiped the call, but he called right back, so I answered the phone.

"Hello," I answered dryly.

"Zyla, I need to come to Virtua in Voorhees. It's your mother, she was in a bad car accident and it's not looking too good," my father said with sadness in his voice. I just knew that I was hearing wrong. I jumped up in a panic trying to find something to put on. I found a pair of tights that I had over Jax's and threw on a t-shirt as the tears fell freely down my face.

"Baby, what's going on? Say something," Jax asked with a concerned tone.

"It's my mom; she was in a car accident. I have to get to the hospital," I cried.

"I'll drive you," Jax stated. After Jax threw on some sweat- pants, we headed out the door. I silently cried the entire ride to the hospital. I kept replaying my last conversation over and over again in my head. I shouldn't have spoken to my mother like that. When we pulled up to the hospital, I hardly waited for Jax to stop the car before I hopped out and ran into the hospital. I spotted my dad in the waiting area and I ran up and hugged him.

"Daddy, what happened? Is mom gonna be okay?" I cried. "I'm not sure, princess. The doctor said she's pretty bad off,

but I haven't even seen her yet," my dad replied with teary eyes. Seeing my father like this was killing me on top of knowing that

MY MOTHER WAS LAID UP IN THE HOSPITAL AND MAY NOT MAKE it. Even though my mom came to Jax's house and disrespected both of us, I still had no right to speak to my mother like that.

"Daddy, I am so sorry. I can't believe that this is happening. I just saw her this morning," I stated. My dad gave me an odd look.

"When did you see your mother?" My father asked.

"This morning, she came over to my boyfriend's house being disrespectful to me and him. Her and I shared some not so nice words then she stormed out. I feel terrible, daddy. I don't know what I will do if something happens to mama. I know we don't always get along, but I still love her," I cried.

"Princess, let's not think about that right now. I'm scared too, but your mama is just fine. She's too stubborn to die without a fight," my dad stated uneasily.

"And what boyfriend do you have?" my dad asked.

"He's over there and his name is Jaxen. I didn't bring him over to meet yet because this isn't how I wanted you to meet him," I told my dad honestly.

"Well, we'll talk about this boyfriend of yours a little later, but for now, call that man over here. Got that man sitting over there like he's visiting another family." I thought about what my dad said, and he was right. I walked over to Jax and grabbed his hand.

"Daddy, this is my boyfriend Jaxen and Jaxen, this is my father Brian, I introduced. They shook hands, but before anything could be said, the doctor came out and walked toward us.

"Family of Davis?" The doctor asked as we gave him our full attention.

"Doctor, is my wife going to be okay?" I didn't like the look in the doctor's face, but I could have just been paranoid.

"I'm sorry we did all that we could, but she had bled out internally," the doctor stated.

I felt like the walls had closed up on me and I couldn't breathe.

I JUST KNEW I HEARD WRONG BUT WATCHING MY FATHER ON HIS knees crying let me know I heard him correctly. I just wasn't willing to accept it. I began to wail loudly and scream for my mom. I was sure that I looked like a crazy woman, but I didn't care what people thought.

After my dad and I cried for what seemed like eternity, we finally mustered up enough strength to go and see my mother's breathless body. When we got back there, Jaxen was right by my side the entire time. Even though my mother looked peaceful in her death, I couldn't help but replay the last words I said to her. Now she's dead, so I'll never get to apologize.

We stayed back there in the room crying and talking to my mom until the funeral home came and took her body. I felt so numb inside that I sat in the chair and rocked in Jaxen's arms as the tears continuously ran down my face. I didn't have a clue how I was gonna explain to Zoey that her grandmother was dead.

Things between me and Mark seemed to be getting serious. We spent damn near every night with one another. I was actually starting to fall for him. Things felt a little weird when I found out he was Zyla's ex. I couldn't believe that Zyla threw her marriage away for a guy like Jax. I mean, don't get me wrong; my baby daddy was fine and could lay some pipe, but he was also a street nigga. Mark, on the other hand, was fine, good in bed, and had a legit job. Not to mention, Mark was consistent and attentive to all my needs.

I just pulled up to Jax's house to drop of Jayla before I went to meet Mark at the bowling alley. I knocked on Jax's door and my eyes damn near popped out of my head when Zyla answered the door. I knew then that Jaxen was in love with her. I tried to keep my hurt under control because I didn't want Zyla to know that I felt some type of way about her. For the first time I took in Zyla's looks and I couldn't deny the fact that she was beautiful with a body to die for. I could see why my baby daddy had fallen for her.

"Hi. Jax will be right down," Zyla stated sweetly. "Hey," I replied.

"Hey, pretty girl. How are you today?" she asked Jayla as we walked into the house.

"Hi Ms. Lala. Is Zoey coming over today?" Jayla asked.

"Maybe tomorrow, she's with her pop-pop right now," Zyla stated softly. I know Mark told me that her mother died from a car crash about a month ago, so I knew she still had to be grieving, but she was doing a great job hiding it.

Jaxen finally made his way downstairs looking like a snack. I knew I had to get out of there quick before I started drooling from the mouth. After Jax hugged and kissed Jayla, she ran up the steps and left the three of us awkwardly looking at one another.

"Well, I'm going to get going," I stated before turning to walk out the door.

"I'll walk you to your car, I need to holla at you about something," Jax said, following behind me. I wasn't sure what the hell he was about to say, but I was ready to hear what it was.

"Yo', I'm not tryna be in your business but you really need to watch out for that nigga Mark. He's not who you think he is."

"You know what, Jax? You really on your bullshit. You just can't stand to see me happy. You got a whole bitch and now you want to control who I'm with? Why because I'm not dick-riding you anymore, Jax?" I yelled.

"You need to lower your fucking voice. I'm telling you this for your own good. Just because we didn't work out as couple, don't mean that I don't care about you. I would never want to see you get hurt," Jaxen stated.

"Your bitch cheated on her husband with you and now you're worried about me getting hurt? You need to worry about your own heart. You're the one fucking with a cheater," I yelled. He had some fucking nerve trying to come at e with that bullshit.

"First off stop calling my girl out of her name and second, you really don't know your man. If that's the story he told you, he's a fucking liar. I know for a fact that he was the one cheating, why the fuck do you think she finally left his ass? So I guess he didn't tell you that he had some other bitch pregnant while he was with Zyla, did he? Did he tell your dumb ass that he wants to be in an open relationship?" Jax shouted. I was standing there pissed off. There was no way in hell we were talking about the same Mark.

"You're such a fucking liar, Jaxen. Get the fuck away from my car," I yelled.

"I tried to warn your dumb ass, but don't come crying to me when you realize who you're really fucking with," Jax stated before walking off, leaving me with my thoughts.

I sat in my car thinking about everything that Jax had just said and that shit really had me in my feelings. My thoughts were all over the place and I didn't know what to think. I mean, I never knew my baby daddy to be a liar, but then again, anything was possible when you're jealous. The only way for me to get answers was to ask Mark

———

I WAS SITTING IN THE DARK ON MY COUCH IN TEARS. I JUST didn't understand why I couldn't find nobody to love me. I wasn't a bad person, so why couldn't I be with someone that was going to flaunt me around and love me unconditionally? My phone alerted me that I had a text message, so I picked it up and saw it was Mark telling me he was on his way. I didn't even respond. I just continued to sip my wine and cry in the dark.

Twenty minutes later, there was a tap at my door, and I knew it was Mark. I got up and slow-walked to the door. Once I opened the door, Mark was standing there looking and smelling so damn good like always. I didn't say anything though. I just turned around and walked away with him following behind me.

"WHAT'S WRONG, BABY? WHY YOU SITTING HERE IN THE DARK?" He asked, turning the lamp on that sat across from the couch. When the lights came on and I looked up at him, I knew he could see the concern in my eyes when he noticed the dried up tears on my face.

"Sasha, what's wrong with you?"

"Mark, I'ma ask you this one time and one time only. Please don't lie to me. Do you have a baby on the way?" I asked.

He sat there for a second trying to get himself together before answering my question. I knew this was before my time, so all he needed to do was answer me and tell me the truth about why he didn't tell me. Then we would be cool.

"Yes, baby, there is, but I'm not sure if it's mine and that's why I never told you. I was trying to wait until I found out. She already messed up my marriage and the baby was probably not mine. Before you ask, it happened when Zyla and I had split for a minute. But I promise you when we got back on good terms, I wasn't messing with this chick. I'm sorry I hurt . I just thought I was saving your heart. I knew we both had been through so much, and we were enjoying each other. The last thing I wanted was to tell you some shit that I don't even know if it's true. I hope this doesn't mess up what we have going on. I promise from here on out I'll keep it real with you no matter what."

It looked like Mark was telling the truth. I just hoped for his sake that he was, because if not, I was done. I couldn't deal with being hurt. I eased my way on Mark's lap and kissed his cheek. I wasn't all the way sure if he was telling me everything, but he did keep it real and let me know that it was a chance of that baby being his.

"You better because I can't take no more hurt, Mark."

"I got you, baby. Now come on and let me take care of you," he said while picking me up bridal style and carrying me up to my room. I laid my head on his shoulder, enjoying the feeling.

MARK

I was sitting in my office talking to Josh about all the shit that had been going on with Kia. I was getting to the point where it was time to get a restraining order on her dumb ass. She was doing all type of shit, but what took the cake was her leaving the note on Sasha's car. I was hoping that Sasha didn't think that note had anything to do with me. I was grateful we were just starting to get back to normal since telling her about the baby. Kia was seven or eight months. I didn't know how far along she was, but what I did know was that she needed to be sitting her crazy ass down somewhere instead of minding my damn business.

"I told you that chick was crazy. She already messed up your marriage and you still don't want her ass, but she still trying. Now, you got this new chick in all your bs. Why didn't you just leave her the hell alone until you got your shit together?"

I knew Josh was right, but it was something about Sasha I just couldn't shake. I was enjoying her and I kind of wanted us to see where this could go. I don't know why I'm feeling like this when I should have been feeling like this with my wife.

"I know, man, but I'm really feeling her. I know you think I'm full of bullshit right now, but I'm serious as fuck, bro," I assured Josh.

"Yeah whatever. How sis doing? When I heard about Mrs. Davis, I was so hurt."

"She not doing too good. When I picked up Zoey the other day, Zyla was walking around like a zombie. She even pulled me in for a hug and I held her tight. She cried in my arms, telling me how her and Mrs. Davis got into an argument the day the accident went down. I told her no matter what they fought about, it wasn't her fault and her mother love her no matter what."

"Damn, what about little mama?"

"Zoey is okay, a little sad but okay. I really feel bad for Mr. Davis. We have to keep Zoey around him for him to function. Every time I pick her up from there, I see the sadness in his eyes. I feel so sorry for him, they were married for so many years. They've been trying to get my ass on the right track with their daughter and I fucked up big time."

"That's crazy, man. I wouldn't know what the hell to do if I lost my wife. She means the world to me, so I feel his pain."

I didn't say anything to that last statement; I just gave Josh a head nod. I was getting tired and ready to go, so while we continued to talk, I gathered my things so I could get ready to head out.

"You finish for the day?" I asked Josh.

"Yeah, I'm about to head out right now. Wifey got a candle-light dinner set up for us, so I can wait to get out of here. What about you, what you about to get into? I hope you heading to the police station to do that restraining order."

Josh was right, but nope, I felt like I could talk to Kia and get her to chill out. When I was with Zyla, all I had to do was show Kia some attention, so I was going to try my luck today.

"I'ma handle that first thing in the morning. Right now I'm going to Sasha's to chill with her since I haven't seen her in a couple of days due to working hard as hell these past couple of days."

"Alright well, I'm out. You better make sure you handle that, bro. Baby girl don't seem stable and you don't want them type problems in your life."

"I am, don't even worry. I got my whole plan in order," I assured Josh. We dapped each other up and he left out my office. As soon as he left out, I grabbed my belongings and did the same. As soon as I got to my car, my phone was ringing and not even looking to see who it was, I picked up on the third ring.

"Hello, this is Mark. How can I help you?"

"Mark, I need you to come to Walmart in Cherry Hill. My car was trashed and I can't even drive it home. Whoever did this left another note telling me she warned me already? Mark, I don't know what type of shit you on, but this has got to stop before it even gets started," Sasha snapped then hung up in my ear.

I hurried and jumped in my car, peeling off. I sped down Route 38 trying to hurry up to get to Sasha to see what's going on. I heard in her voice that she was real upset. When she mentioned the letter, I automatically knew who it was. Kia was doing way to much and I was getting sick of her ass. Ten minutes later, I was pulling up into the Walmart parking lot. I looked around until I saw a couple of cop cars. Then I spotted Sasha talking to one of them. I drove over to where they were, parked my car and jumped right out. I gave Sasha her space while she talked to the police, and made my way over to her car. All the windows were smashed out and the tires were flat. All I could do was shake my head, Kia's ass was doing the most and the shit was getting crazy.

"Come on, Mark. I'm ready to go," Sasha said with an attitude. I knew she was pissed off, so I didn't say anything. I just walked to my car and opened the door for her. When she got in, I

MADE SURE SHE WAS ALL THE WAY IN, AND CLOSED THE DOOR. Once I got in and buckled up, I looked over to her.

"I'ma have my mechanic come get your car so he can fix it by tomorrow."

"My car is straight. I already called Jax and he has it taken care of." I don't know why what she said rubbed me the wrong way, but it did.

"Why the fuck would you call him, Sasha? I would have made sure your car got fixed. If we gone be dealing with each other, you don't have to call him for shit. Unless it has to do with his daughter."

Sasha turned and looked at me with an attitude. I knew what she was about to say was going to piss me off even more just by her demeanor.

"First of all, Jax and I have the same mechanic, and he always makes sure my car is straight because his daughter has to ride around in it. Mark, right now, we are just starting, and I need you to understand that it's nothing between me and Jax. We do nothing but co-parent, but if I need anything, he always has my back and vice versa. We remain friends to be better parents to our child," Sasha said then turned to look out the window.

I wasn't going to say shit. I was just gone drop her ass off and keep it moving. I had to go handle Kia then I would come back to deal with Sasha.

I had a very eventful day, now this baby was kicking and moving all over the place. I really wasn't feeling good, so I figured I would come home to relax. I had just come from Walmart's parking lot and I was sitting in my car watching the cops come and everything. I even saw Mark come to that bitch's rescue, but when I called, he doesn't even answer the damn phone. A loud knock at my door had me jumping out my seat. The knocked was so loud I thought it was the police but when I opened the door,

Mark was standing there looking at me with the meanest mug on his face.

"Well, hello, baby daddy. What do I owe the pleasure of this visit?" I smiled and he pushed his way in.

"You fucking bitch!" Mark snapped while turning to face me. I looked at him, laughing hysterically. I didn't give a fuck about his attitude. He should have been come over here to check on me. Why did it have to take for me to trash one of his little bitches cars for him to give me some attention?

"So... I finally got your attention, huh? By the way, Sasha is pretty but she ain't me," I giggled.

· · ·

"Yeah, I know she ain't you because ya ass crazy as hell. Why the fuck you won't leave me the fuck alone, and go on with your life?"

"News flash, nigga. I'm seven and a half months pregnant with your damn child. See, this is why the shit that's happening to you is happening to you. When you were married, I dealt with the bullshit. I was okay with playing second, but I ain't playing second to no new bitch, Mark. It's either me and your baby or you won't be happy with no fucking body and I mean that on my unborn child. See, Mark you fucked with the wrong heart. I waited for you to break up with your wife thinking we were going to be one big happy family."

"Kia, I never had no intentions on being more then what we were. I don't know how you went from us just fucking to us being a happy family. You were just the side bitch, ma. Nothing more, nothing less."

All I saw was rage in his face right before he wrapped both his hands around my throat. The more I smiled, the harder he squeezed. I grabbed and pulled at his hands, trying to get him to loosen up, but he wouldn't stop. I felt like I was going to pass out, but he let me go, causing me to fall to the floor. I was so hurt by what he just did to me, I just laid on the floor and cried.

"Look what you made me do. If you keep this crazy shit up, Kia, I'ma kill your ass and I mean it," Mark snapped before heading out of the door.

I was so damn big I could barely get off the damn floor. I had to roll on my knees and crawl over to the couch so I could have something to pull up on. As soon as I stood up all the way, I felt warm fluid trickling down my legs. The tears started running down my face instantly, because I knew it was too soon for me to be having this baby. I was further along than my past pregnancies, but I was still scared to death. I called Mark, and of course, he didn't answer.

So, I had no choice but to call Kesha. I knew she would be mad at me, but I knew she would come right away. After I called the paramedics, I called Kesha. I was having this baby today and it's was no reason to worry because it wasn't something I could change. The paramedics were knocking at the door but there was no way in hell, I would make it to the door with the pain that I was in.

"It's open!" I yelled in pain. The paramedics started asking all of these questions, and if I weren't in so much pain, I would have smacked one of their asses. I was in too much pain to answer any of their questions. All I wanted them to do was get me to the hospital, so I could check on my baby. Just as they were putting me in the ambulance, Kesha was walking up. She decided to ride with me in the ambulance. I couldn't lie; I was really glad that she was with me because I felt so alone and unwanted.

As soon as we got to the hospital, they took me straight to the back. The nurse came in and hooked me up to all these machines. I instantly got scared because I remember this shit all to well. I had lost a couple of babies and I was so sure this pregnancy was fine since I carried this one the longest.

"Is my baby okay? I'm not due yet," I asked in a panic.

"Try to stay calm. The doctor will be in soon to check everything out," the nurse assured me.

"Oh God!" I cried out in pain as the sharp pains shot through my belly.

"Kia, everything is gonna be okay, and I'm gonna be right here to help you through this. Did you want me to try to call Mark for you?" Kesha said.

"He won't answer, I tried to call just before I called you," I told her sadly.

"I'll call him from my phone to see if he'll answer," Kesha told me. The doctor came in and checked my cervix.

"Okay, we're gonna prep you to have this baby. You're dilated eight centimeters, so this baby could be coming anytime. Do you know the sex of the baby?"

"No, I wanted it to be a surprise," I replied.

"Well the suspense will be over soon." The doctor walked over to the baby screen and looked at the scribbly lines that was on the paper.

"I need an ultrasound machine in here as soon as possible. These lines are showing some distress," the doctor told the nurse. The nurse left out and came back with the machine. The doctor performed the ultrasound and told me he had to perform a c- section, which was the one thing that I didn't want. On the way to the operating room, Kesha called Mark from her phone.

"Hi Mark, this is Kesha, I'm Kia's sister. I was calling to inform you that Kia is about to give birth just in case you wanted to come up here for the delivery. She has to have a c-section and we're at Cooper hospital," she told him before hanging up.

"What did he say?" I asked.

"Fuck him, sis. He's not coming, but don't worry, I got you. Now let's go meet your baby," my sister stated, causing me to give a slight smile. She was right. Fuck Mark.

My cell phone ringing brought me out of my daze, I looked at my phone and it was Jax calling so I swiped the call. I wasn't in the mood to talk to him right now. It hadn't been long since my mom died, and I often found myself shutting the world out. Today was one of those days for me. I was glad that Zoey was with Mark today because all I wanted to do was be by myself. Losing my mother put a major strain on me and Jaxen's relationship. I rarely answered his calls or the door when he came by. I still felt so guilty about my last words to my mother, and the fact that we were arguing over her not wanting me with Jax didn't make me feel any better. I heard my phone ding, indicating I had a text. I was almost sure it was Jax without looking at my phone.

Jax: Zyla, I know you see me calling you. I'm not sure what's going on with you, but I'm doing all I can to be there for you in any way you need me to be.

Me: Jax, I just need some time. I need to be by myself right now.

Jax: Zyla, what the fuck are you trying to say? Are you saying you need time today? or are you speaking in general?

Jax: I'm talking about in general. I'm just in a bad place right now and feel like I need to be alone. I need to properly grieve over my mother, if that's okay with you?

Jax: You know what, Zyla? Do what the fuck you want to do. I'm so tired of every time you get in one of your funky ass moods, you get rude and push me away. It's one thing to grieve, but it's another thing to act like a total bitch. You do you, Zyla and I'll do me. I'm tired of always chasing after your ass. Have a nice fucking day.

I read Jaxen's text about three times in disbelief. I couldn't

believe he had the nerve to speak to me like that. My blood was boiling so bad. I was lounging in my bra and panties, but I was about to throw something on, go next door and give Jax's a piece of my mind because he had the game fucked up. I threw on a t-shirt and tights and stormed out the door.

Bang Bang Bang...

I pounded on Jax's door like I was the police and he snatched the door open like a mad man.

"Zyla, why the fuck are you banging on my door like that? And why the fuck are you at my door if you need so much time alone?"

"Jaxen, you really need to watch who the fuck you're talking to like that? So now I'm a bitch?" I yelled all in my emotions.

"Zyla, your ass doesn't fucking listen. I said you're acting like a bitch; there's a difference. Every time shit don't go your way, you want to push me away like I'm a nobody. Then I have to chase your ass, but I'm not doing that shit this time. I love you, but I won't get treated like shit when I didn't do anything to you. I'm not your problem, Zyla, but I am trying to be the solution," Jax stated.

"Jax, are you sure that you're not the problem because last I checked me, and my mama argued over me being with you? Now she's not here, Jax. She's gone because I wanted to be with you. If I would have just stayed away from you, maybe she would still be here!" I yelled, crying hysterically. "She walked out your door, trying to convince me to leave you alone and I choose you and now she's dead!" I yelled again. But after the look that appeared on Jaxen's face, I immediately wish I didn't say it.

"You know what, Zyla? Fuck you! For you to sit there and blame me for your mama's death is crazy. Remember this, you weren't here only because I wanted you here. You were here because this is where you wanted to be. If you want me to leave you alone, then I will. Shit, I was doing better when I was just fucking chicks and keeping it moving. Maybe falling for your spoiled, stuck-up ass was wrong. You can go, ma and don't ever knock on my door the fuck again." Jax barked before shutting the door in my face.

I was so hurt that I just stood there staring at Jax's door with falling tears. Jaxen had never spoken to me like that, so I didn't know how to handle it. I was sorry that I hurt his feelings, but that's how I felt. Jax slammed the door in my face, leaving me standing there looking dumb. I ran back home to sit on my couch and ended up crying myself to sleep. I regretted what I said and maybe I did need to be alone.

Baby Marquis turned one month today. That's right; I had a baby boy. Mark bitch ass never came to the hospital, but he has stopped by twice since I've been home. I couldn't understand how he loves his daughter but not his son. I knew I wasn't his wife when I conceived Marquis, but we were fucking around hot and heavy. Mark wasn't paying us any attention because he was too busy playing house with that bitch Sasha and her daughter. I knew I had to do something about that bitch. It was no way I was gonna sit around and let her take the man that I felt was rightfully mine.

"Kia, you don't hear the baby screaming?" Kesha yelled, breaking me from my thoughts.

"I zoned out for a second. Give me a break, Kesha," I told her. "Kia, you really need to get your shit together. You have a son,

and instead of you being a mother to your child, you keep leaving him in the room by himself crying while you waste your time on thinking about his no good daddy. Kia, you need to let Mark go and move on. It's clear that he doesn't want you or the baby!" Kesha yelled but it was something about what Kesha said that pissed me off and caused me to snap. I charged at her fast, swinging wildly.

"Bitch, are you crazy?" Kesha yelled, screaming loudly while delivering some powerful punches to my face. Hell, I didn't realize that she had hands. Before I knew it, I was on the floor and she was on top of me pinning me down.

"You know what, Kia? I don't know what happened to you but you really need to get your shit together for the sake of the baby. You so busy worrying about Mark that you forgot that you have a son that needs and wants you. Mark may not be here but I have been here for you since day one and you have the nerve to swing on me because you don't like what I said? Well, you're on your own now. I decided to work it out with Joe so I won't be back," Kesha stated, getting up and storming out the door.

I was so pissed that I couldn't even think straight, and the baby screaming wasn't making things any better. I snatched up my phone and called Mark's phone over and over again, but he still didn't answer. I had some shit I needed to handle. I didn't hear the baby crying, so I walked into his room to see if he was sleep. I was surprised to see that Kesha's husband, Joe, holding Marquis and feeding him. I just rolled my eyes and walked past the room. Kesha was right; I was so busy chasing Mark that I wasn't being the mother that I needed to be.

Everyone had left and it was just me and my son left in the house. It was a little after one, so I decided to call Mark one last time and surprisingly, he answered.

"Kia, why the fuck do you keep blowing up my phone like I don't have a job? What the fuck is the emergency?"

"I didn't mean to bother you at work. It's just you haven't been over to see your son. Mark, our son really needs you. Why can't we just be a happy family?" I cried into the phone.

"Kia, I don't know how many times I have to tell you this. I've moved on. There is no me and you. Once I get the baby tested, if it turns out that he's mine, then of course I'll be there for my son. What type of father do you think I am? But I really need to go. And Kia, please don't call me again until after the DNA test proves that I'm the father," Mark stated before disconnecting the call. I was so pissed that I screamed loudly. I put on some sneakers and peeked in on my son's room to make sure he was still sleeping. Since Joe had just fed him and I had just changed him. I figured he would be good until I made a quick stop. I knew I shouldn't have left him alone, but I needed to get our family back.

I jumped in my car and headed over to his little bitch Sasha's house. I wasn't sure what I was going to do when I got there, but I knew she wouldn't be with my man anymore after today. I parked my car and knocked on the door several times before Sasha finally came to the door.

"Hi, may I help you?" she asked.

"Yeah, you can start by leaving my man alone. Mark and I have a son and you're in the way of us being happy."

"You have a lot of fucking nerve showing up at my door. I'm not stopping you from being happy. If Mark wanted you, he would be with you."

I rushed her into the house and we both hit the floor. After scrambling around on the floor, I managed to climb on top of her and get a few good punches in before she was able to overpower me.

"Get the fuck out of my house, you crazy bitch?" Sasha yelled, hitting me once more. I managed to pull out my blade and I charged at Sasha again but this time with every hit, I was slicing her up. I barely knew who I was at this point. I started to see blood and instead of feeling sad, I sliced her even more. Sasha's screams fell on deaf ears. I sliced her face and she yelled in pain, so I did it again. Before I knew it, I was stabbing her all over her body and blood was everywhere. It was like I blacked out and turned into a crazy woman.

"Freeze! Put the weapon down!" an officer yelled. I couldn't believe I had stabbed Sasha and was now about to go to jail. All I could do at this point was cry because reality had now kicked in. I looked down and Sasha wasn't moving so I dropped the blade and surrendered. The officer cuffed me and put me in his cop car. I was scared and needed someone to go get my son because he was home alone.

When the cops put me in the cop car, I noticed that Sasha's neighbors were all standing around watching me being hauled off. I guess all the noise we were making, especially Sasha's screaming, was heard by the neighbors and someone called the police. I couldn't do shit but put my head down. What the fuck have I done? All the blood and slashes on her skin, I knew I was going down for attempted murder.

Twenty minutes later, we were walking into the police station, and that's when it hit me that the baby was alone.

"Please, I need to make a phone call," I yelled.

"Sweetheart, you just got here. You have to wait until you make it to central booking, then that's when you'll get your one phone call."

"I need it now, ma'am. My one-month old son is home alone." I explained to the lady cop that was at the desk.

"I'm not supposed to do this, but give me the number." I raddled off Mark's number to her and she called him. She gave me a head nod that she had reached him. I was thankful for this older lady. I felt a little better knowing that someone was in the way to pick my baby up. I couldn't believe my actions. What the hell is wrong with me?

I was picking Jayla up from school because Sasha's ass never picked her up. My ass was so furious. What the fuck could she have been doing for her to miss picking my daughter up?

"Daddy, where is mommy at?"

"Baby, she had to handle something and got busy. She didn't mean to be late," I explained to her, not wanting her to feel any type of way. As soon as I hopped in the car and made sure Jayla was straight, my phone began to ring. I picked it right up not even looking to see who it was.

"Hello, may I speak to Jaxen Taylor." "Hello, this is he."

"This is Nurse Clarey calling from Kennedy Hospital. We have Sasha Pierce here in our care. Your name was down as her emergency contact. Can you please come now? We have her stable, but she's been hurt really bad."

I didn't even know what to say or do. I was scared and praying nothing happened to her seriously. Jayla wouldn't even be able to take it if something happened to her mama. I told the nurse I was on my way. Then I dialed the only person I trusted Jayla with other then Khi or G-mom. I hadn't talked to her in about a month, so I hoped she answered for me. I dialed Zyla's number and she picked up on the first ring.

"Hello, Jax," she said, sounding drowsy.

"Hey, ma. I know it's been a minute, but I need a huge favor. I need you to keep Jayla for me, and I promise I'll be right over to get her when I'm finished taking care of business."

"Sure, bring her over. Zoey and I just woke up from a nap anyway. I'm about to make us something to eat for dinner."

"Alright, I'll be there shortly, and thanks so much. I'll explain everything when I get there." I peeled off, trying to make it to Zyla's crib in record-breaking time. Ten minutes later, I was pulling up, and she was standing in the doorway waiting for me.

"Ms. Lala!" Jayla screamed while she ran up on the step and right into Zyla's arms. It had been a little minute since Jayla and I both saw her. She was dressed down in her sweats and an over- sized t-shirt. She had her hair up in a messy bun just like she used to do when she was just chillin'. I swear I missed this girl with all my heart.

"Hey, baby. Go ahead in the house with Zoey; she's in her room," Zyla said. I knew she could sense something serious was wrong because it was all in my face. Before I could even speak, I couldn't control myself. I pulled her into my arms and held her tight.

"Thank you so much for this. I have to get to the hospital; some-thing happened to Sasha."

"Oh my God! Is she okay?" Zyla asked in a concern tone.

"They said she's stable but that she was just hurt really bad. So, I guess that's a good thing. I just know I couldn't take Jayla with me because I wasn't sure what I was walking into."

"Ok, baby. I got you. Go ahead and handle your business and if you wanna talk when you come back, we can do that. I miss you so damn much, Jax." Zyla yelled before walking away.

"I miss you too, beautiful," I said, winking at her. I would be lying if I said I didn't miss her like crazy, but I needed to show her that she wasn't going to keep playing with a nigga's feelings. I wanted her and needed her like the air I breathe. I knew sooner or later we would cross paths again and now I know we were definitely meant to be.

———

SASHA HAD SUFFERED FROM SO MANY STABBED WOUNDS IT WAS crazy. Especially the ones on her face and she would need some surgery to get rid of the scars. I sat there until she woke up and she told me everything that happened. I wanted so bad to beat the shit out of Mark and kill that crazy bitch Kia. Sasha could have lost her life to this bullshit. All because this nigga wanna play with people's feelings. All the way to Zyla's house, I was trying to figure out a way to fuck her baby daddy up without her hating me, but I couldn't seem to think of a plan. I guess she would just have to be mad at me for a little bit.

After sitting up at the hospital for hours with Sasha, I promised her I would be back up tomorrow. Now I was pulling up in front of Zyla's house. I was so exhausted and all I wanted to do was climb in the bed with her. I hope she had gotten Jayla ready for bed and put her right in the room with Zoey. I know we needed to talk, and we could do that laying right next to each other. I parked my car in my driveway then walked over to Zyla's crib. The minute I made it up on the step, the front door flew opened.

"You were waiting on a nigga, huh?" I said with a big smile on my face.

"Of course, I was," Zyla said, pulling me into the house.

"Where the kids at?"

"They're sleep...it took me a little longer with Jayla. It's like she sensed something was wrong. How is Sasha?" Zyla asked in concern.

"She's fucked up, but she'll be okay. She may need a little cosmetic surgery due to the cuts on her face. Apparently, Kia went over there going on a rampage about how Sasha won't leave her man alone. Talking about she was messing up her family. That chick clearly was out of her mind. I wonder if he was still dealing with her while dealing with Sasha. I tried to tell her to leave that nigga alone, but she wasn't listening to me and now look," I said in so much anger.

"Shhh...baby, you getting a little loud. I don't wanna wake the girls up. Are you hungry?"

"Not really. I just want something to drink and to lay next to you. Is that cool with you?" I asked.

"Yes, that's fine. Go ahead to the room, make yourself comfortable, and I'll bring you some iced tea."

"Ok, baby. Thanks again," I said, leaning in to kiss her forehead.

I walked off to the bedroom and stopped in to peek at the girls. They were both knocked out sleeping. They were both so pretty and I swear I would do anything in my power to make sure they both were good for the rest of their lives. The shit with Sasha had me so fucking scared. All I keep thinking about is what if I had to tell my daughter her mama was dead. I'm a straight hood nigga, but I wouldn't have been able to deal with that bullshit at all.

Once I made it to the room, I stripped out of my clothes and climbed right in the bed. I stared out of the window, thanking the big man in the sky for sparing Sasha's life. She may not have been my woman anymore, but she was the mother of my child and a good one at that. We may not agree on everything, but she's always been good with Jayla, and for that, I will always respect her. The feeling of the bed moving and Zyla wrapping her small arms around my waist caused a smile to creep up on my face. I knew we had shit to work out, but this right here was the best feeling ever.

MARK

The shit that Kia did had me pacing the floor all night long. Not to mention this little boy was crying all night. He shut up long enough to eat, then he was back at it. I called Kesha to come get him, but the bitch hung up on me and told me I needed to bond with my son. I don't know what these bitches didn't understand, I wasn't claiming this baby until I got it tested. Since Kia was on some crazy psycho shit, I was forced to be his daddy right now, even if I wasn't. The cries were driving me crazy, so I decided to go to the one person that I knew would be able to help me with this. I knew she wouldn't be happy to see me, but I knew she wouldn't turn the baby away. Zyla had a good heart. Even though the shit hurt her, I knew she would still accept the baby because of it possibly being Zoey's brother.

Once I pulled up in front of the house, I was happy to see her car there. I sat for a minute, but as soon as Marquis woke up, he started crying once again. I jumped out of the car, grabbed his car seat and went straight up the steps to the house that was once mine. As soon as I was about to open the door, it flew open.

"Mark, what the fuck are you doing here?" Zyla asked while looking behind her back like she was looking out for somebody.

"I need your help...he won't stop crying," I said with sad eyes. "Nigga, I know you lying. You did not come over here for me to help with the mistress' baby. Mark, get the fuck off my damn step." Zyla yelled.

She tried to close the door, but I placed my foot at the entrance, stopping her from closing the door. The mean mug on her face showed me that she was agitated. I knew I was wrong for this, but I didn't have no one else to turn too.

"Zyla, please. I know I fucked up, but I don't have no one else to help me."

"Where's that crazy bitch's family at? I know she got a sister, why you didn't go to her damn house? It's nothing I can do to help you here.

"Baby, what's going on?" Jax asked, walking up to the door. "Everything is fine," Zyla said, trying to push Jax back.

"Go in the house and tend to the girls and let me talk to this sucka ass nigga," Jax retorted. Shockingly Zyla didn't say shit, she walked off just like a small child listening to her daddy. The shit had my mind gone. My ex was soft as shit, but when she was with me, she would have cursed me the fuck out. What has this dude turned her into?

"Man, this has nothing to do with you," I said annoyed as fuck. "Nigga, this has everything to do with me when you show up at my woman's crib. Truth be told, little man saved your life, because I owe you an ass whooping. My daughter's mama is in the hospital bed all fucked up because of you and your bullshit. When will you learn that woman are meant to be loved and cherished? They're not supposed to be going through heartache and pain. Stay the fuck away from Zyla and Sasha!" Jax barked.

"Man, you sound really dumb. Zyla and I have a kid together and Sasha is a grown ass woman. If she doesn't want to see me anymore, she will tell me, but until then, I will continue to see her."

"Mark, leave 'for I forget where the fuck I'm at and kill ya stupid ass, and that's some real shit." The look in his eyes told me that he was serious, and I had to think about the baby and Zoey, so I just walked off, hopping in my car and feeling defeated. I made my way back home to feed the baby and hopefully get him to take a nap, so I can shower.

———

I HAD GOTTEN JOSH AND HIS WIFE TO KEEP MARQUIS FOR ME while I went to the hospital to check on Sasha. I knew I should have been up there by her side when this first went down, but I couldn't because I had the baby. The last thing I wanted to do was flaunt the baby in her face when the baby's mother was the reason for her lying in this hospital bed. Once I made it to the hospital, I went to the desk, gave Sasha's name, and they handed me a pass. When I made it to her room, I stood outside of the door, not knowing how she was holding up. I was mad at myself for letting this happened. I should have gone ahead, got the restraining order and made sure that Sasha knew that Kia was crazy. I should have just told her everything that Kia was doing so she could have been more careful. I walked in her room and looked at all the bandages that covered her. Especially the ones that were all over her face. Sasha was wrapped like a mummy and it was all because of me.

"You see what your bitch did to me?" Sasha asked in a low tone, but that didn't stop the venom that dripped from her voice. I knew she was pissed, and she had every right to be.

"Sasha...baby, I'm so sorry. I didn't know she was crazy. I didn't know this was going to happen."

"Was she the one that put the notes on my car? Was she the one that trashed my car?" Sasha asked while I just stood there in a daze.

"Baby, please just forgive me. I swear I didn't know this was going to happen. I had no idea she would go this far."

"Mark, save your apologies and answer my fucking questions.

IS SHE THE FUCKING ONE!" Sasha yelled. "Yes..." I said just above a whisper.

"Mark, get the fuck out of my room and lose my number. My life and peace are more important than dealing with this shit. Get the fuck out and don't ever contact me again."

The room door opened, so I turn to see who it was and was met face to face with Jax. I was so sick of this dude I wish his ass would just disappear.

"I thought I told you to stay the fuck away from her. You seem not to listen!" Jax barked.

"Jax, calm down. He was just leaving," Sasha said. I turned around, looked at Sasha and apologized once more. When she didn't respond, I walked out of the door — not expecting for Jax to follow behind me.

"Look, man. I'm trying my hardest to let you live because of ya little girl. The shit hard to do, since you don't listen."

"Like I told you before, homeboy. I do what the fuck I want," I snapped, growing angry over this situation. I went to turn away, but before I got a chance to, Jax punched me right in my face. I hit the floor, and everything went black. I guess you could say I deserved this shit, because, at this point, I really did feel like it.

I
t had been a couple of weeks since Jax and I had been going strong. He had even gotten me into some therapy for my mama's death, and I was dealing with it just fine. Tons of life-changing situations had been going on in the past six months, and the therapist said I was on the verge of having a mental break. I may have thought I was handling everything well, but deep inside, I wasn't. I had gotten through a divorce, jumped in a new relationship, started school, and lost my mother all in a months' time. I had been honest with the therapist and told her that Mark and I had been out of love for years, so it really wasn't nothing getting involved with Jax.

"Hey, honey. You sitting in here quiet," my daddy said while walking into the living room.

"Hey, old man. How are you feeling?" I got up and pulled him in for a hug.

"I'm feeling good since I've been going to the sessions. How about you?" He asked.

"Daddy, I'm finally feeling like myself again. Thanks to Jax." My daddy and I haven't talked much about my relationships.

He usually stays out of my business unless I come to him with a problem. That's why we had a great relationship; he would let me live my life and learn from it unlike my mother. She always had a say so and wanted my life to run the way she wanted it, not how I wanted it to. *She was the mama and whatever she said went,* I thought with a huge smile on my face.

"So, you really feeling him, huh?" My daddy asked.

"Yes, I've been feeling him, but I couldn't come out with it because I was a married woman. Mark and I been unhappy, but I tried to make it work for Zoey and mama, I guess. Jax was the one that showed me how a man was really supposed to treat a woman. I know I saw it in you ever since I was little, but I also saw the bad. Mama always told me that when you get married, you make it work no matter what. I guess I listened to that and ran with it. Then I was always thinking Zoey would grow up wrong if she wasn't bought up in a two-parent home."

"I'm sorry you stayed in that bad relationship so long, baby girl. I should have been more involved, but I figured your mother stayed in your business enough. I wasn't too proud of the life I heard Jax lives, but I see he's a good man. He also assured me that he was working on better goals in life. Once he told me that, I opened up a little and now he's growing on me. As long as he makes you happy and keeps you and my grandbaby safe, he doesn't have anything to worry about," my daddy chuckled and I smiled at him.

"I love you, daddy!" I said while kissing his cheek.

"I love you too, baby girl. Now, why don't you go in that kitchen and cook ya old man some dinner. I had already taken some pork-chops out, but I don't feel like cooking."

"I got you. I might as well call Jax and tell him to come over with the girls."

After I called Jax, I made my way into my mama's kitchen and looked around for a minute before I got dinner started. I missed her so fucking much, and many nights, I still cried about her death. I didn't blame myself or Jax anymore, because I knew she was in a car accident that none of us had any control over. Did I wish we were on better terms when she died? Yes but I also knew she loved me no matter who I was with. She may have been mad, but she would have gotten over it. I pushed all the thoughts I was having to the back of my mind and got dinner started.

———

I WAS LYING IN MY BED LOOKING UP AT THE CEILING. I WAS finally getting better at trying to enjoy life. I was almost finished with my classes since I started going hard online. Graduation was coming, and I still didn't know my plans. Jax had a couple of plans lined up for himself and he said I can jump along on his, but I still needed to figure out something of my own. Something I would be able to fall back on in case of something did not work out. I know I shouldn't think that way, but this was life shit happened all the time.

"What you in here thinking about?" Jax asked while climbing on top of me, causing me to giggle.

"Just trying to figure out what my goal is when I finish school." "How about you chill a little bit after school, let me fly you around the world and show you what you been missing? Then when we get back, we could figure out what you gone do together,"

Jax asked with a smile on his face.

"Baby, I can't go all around the world. What will I do with Zoey?" I asked.

"Your daddy and her daddy. I already talked to your dad and I know her daddy don't mind keeping her. Plus, you need to get away, babe. Let me show you a good time."

"Ok. I guess we could do it. I don't remember the last time my ass got on a plane. Mark would always be on business trips and I would be here with Zoey, so I could use a vacation. I swear I love you," I said, meaning every word of it. Jax then kissed my forehead before working his way to my lips. Then he eased his way down to my breasts, making sure to show them both attention. I moaned out in pleasure, enjoying Jaxen like I always did. He was now face to face with my pussy, sending chills through my body just knowing what was about to happen.

"You ready for me to taste that thing, ma?" Jax asked, causing me to moan out once more.

After he let me know what he was about to do, he started sucking on my clit gently, causing my juices to start running out of me instantly. Jax had my body doing all type of shit. I felt him as he eased his finger in my wetness, while he flicked his tongue across my clit rapidly. The friction from what Jax was doing to me caused my body to jerk, and right then and there, I knew I was having my first orgasm of the night. I closed my eyes for a second to enjoy every bit of it.

"So, you gone fall asleep on me since you got yours?" Jax asked while licking his lips.

"No, I wouldn't do that to you," I said, pulling him in for a kiss while wrapping my arms around his neck. I felt Jax manhood poking at my tunnel. He gave me an intense stare as he eased his way in me nice and slow. After he was all the way in, he hit me with deep, slow, and long strokes. Jax was so in tune with my body and the shit was feeling amazing.

"Fuck, ma. This shit feels so damn good," Jax moaned in my ear while hitting that spot I never knew I had.

"Yesss, baby! It feels so good. I think I'm about to cum. Baby, can you cum with me?" I moaned out while I was cummin' all over Jax. Our bodies shook together as we both came long and hard.

"You good, beautiful?" Jax asked.

"Yes, baby. I'm great, thanks to you," I cooed while Jax pulled me into his arms. We both stared at each other until we dozed off.

I

t's only been two weeks since I've gotten out of the hospital and although I was doing much better, I was still in a lot of pain. I hated to look in the mirror because my face was pretty fucked up. I was so grateful for my best friend Amanda and Jaxen. They really been coming through for me. Jax was paying for my much needed surgery, and I couldn't wait because I couldn't bear to look at myself in the mirror. I never thought I'd see the day when I would say this but I had even grown to like Zyla. Zyla was a sweet woman with a good heart, and I could see why Jaxen had fallen so hard for her. Even she played a big part in my recovery. She kept Jayla while Jaxen came to visit, and she even helped me out with a few things. I didn't blame her for leaving Mark's dumb ass. There's not a day that goes by that I don't wish I had listened to Jax when he tried to warn me about Mark but no, I was too busy looking for someone to love me.

"Sasha, you really need to snap out of this funk that you're in, I know that shit doesn't seem like it's gonna get better, but it will," Amanda stated, breaking me from my thoughts.

"Amanda, that all sounds good but look at me that bitch Kia ruined my life I'll be scar forever. Who's gonna wanna look at a body that's sliced up? Tell me that Amanda since you have all the answers," I said with tears in my eyes.

"A fucking man that's looking for a great woman and with a big heart. Yes, your face doesn't look exactly like how it used to, but you're still beautiful inside and out. Once you recover from your surgery, you really gonna be the shit. Guess what if all else fails and those niggas don't know they found themselves a real bitch, fuck them. Hell... I'll be your girlfriend if a real man don't snatch your ass up," Amanda stated, serious as hell. All I could do was laugh loudly. Amanda sure knew how to turn a frown upside down.

"You laughing but, bitch I'm serious. I'll chill on you for now and see if you find the man of your dreams. The first thing you gonna do is let him find you. Don't go looking for a soul, but until you find the right one, you better hoe it out with your bestie."

"Bitch, your ass is crazy. Ain't nobody trying to be no damn hoe at this age and speaking of hoeing, when are you gonna settle down?" I asked her. Amanda was a good woman, but she was a tad bit on the wild side. I knew she just needed the right man to get her on track.

"Bitch, I don't know. I just can't take these niggas serious, but that's enough about me. This is about you talking crazy like it's the end of the world. I promise you'll find someone that treats you like the queen you are," she assured me.

———

LATER THAT NIGHT, I WAS IN THE DOORWAY, AND MY EYES landed on Mark. I hadn't seen him since the day Jaxen beat his ass at the hospital, and the truth was, I was mad that I had to see him now. I couldn't lie and say that I didn't miss him, but I knew after what happened to me, I would never lay down with him again. I've been staying at Jaxen's house ever since I was released from the hospital. Jaxen and Zyla insisted that I stay at Jaxen's until I was fully healed, and I didn't see a problem with it since Jax damn near lived with

Zyla. I guess Mark was coming to pick up Zoe since Zyla and Jax were leaving for vacation in the morning.

"Sasha, I know I'm the last person you want to but can you please just hear me out? Please I swear to make it quick and then you'll never have to worry about me again," Mark pleaded. Against my better judgment, I caved.

"You have three minutes, Mark. Nothing more and I mean, nothing," I told him.

"I am truly sorry for what I allowed to happen to you. I wish I was there to stop it. I know this don't mean shit now, but I truly was serious if I could be honest. I was falling for you, Sasha. I fucked up big time. You were the second great woman I hurt and let get away. Take care, Sasha. I'll never forget you," Mark confessed me before walking away.

As much as I missed him, I could never fuck with him again. I just couldn't allow a man like him back in my space. My peace was ruined, and I'd rather have that back then just be with someone to keep from being alone. I was going to take Amanda's good advice and stop looking and wait for Mr. Right to find me.

"Thank you, Mark. I really appreciate you apologizing, and I forgive you, but I could never fuck with you like that. You have a nice life," I sassed right before walking back in the house. I wasn't sure if I needed to hear that or not, but when I got back in the house, it felt like the weight of the world had been lifted off my shoulder. Right then and there, I decided to let go and let God. Things happen for a reason, and I believe this was my calling to sit back and learn my worth. Life would get better for me. I just had to be patient and let it all fall into place.

Things had been crazy in my life lately, but I was learning to deal with it. I never not once thought I would be raising a baby alone, but here I am. At first, all he did was cry all the time, but after a few days, he was good. I guess he had to get used to me just like I had to get used to him. Kia had been calling my phone, but I refused to talk to her crazy ass. Kesha did eventually start watching him for me while I went to work, but she made it very clear that she would drop him off at my job if I even acted like I wasn't coming back for him.

I was in my living room thinking about how my entire life went left in a matter of months. I lost my family then jumped into another relationship. Then I lost her too because my possible baby mama went crazy and stabbed up Sasha. Now her crazy ass is in jail, leaving me to raise a kid that may not even be mine, but that's what happens when you fuck over the people that love you the most. I took the DNA the day after I went to pick the baby up from Kia's crib. I needed to know was this baby mine, because her batshit crazy ass definitely wasn't capable of raising no damn baby. The results should be back any day now, and I'm just waiting patiently. Apart of me was hoping he was mine. I've had him for almost a month now and the little fella definitely grew on me. It was kinda cool having a son and Zoey was so good with him. I had just dropped him off with Kesha and now I was walking into my office. Once I made it in, I spoke to everyone and grabbed a cup of coffee before heading to my office.

———

It was now the afternoon and I just got back from lunch. I was in my office checking my emails and catching up on paperwork. Since I had taken a week off from work to keep Zoey, while Zyla and her punk ass nigga decided to take a vacation. I already had baby Marquis, so I made the best of it. I did a little work from home, but I couldn't do but so much with a newborn on my hip. I heard a light knock on the door before the door opened.

"Hey, Josh. Wassup?" I asked Josh as he walked in and closed the door.

"Not much, but I figured you would want this," Josh replied, waving the envelope that was in his hand.

"When did it come?" I asked.

"While you were out to lunch, I went to get my mail from the mailbox, so I figured I would grab yours. When I saw where it came from. I figured I would bring it right in," Josh said.

My heart started pounding knowing it was the DNA results. That letter was gonna change my life forever rather he's mine or not. I got up from my desk and took the envelope out of Josh's hand. Josh was about to leave out the office but I stopped him. Josh was the only friend I had and I needed him here when I read the results.

I didn't waste no time ripping the envelope open, as soon as I read the results tears flooded my eyes. I couldn't believe that my entire life was flipped upside down for a baby that wasn't even mine. I felt like a stupid bitch ass nigga, but it was what it was. I finally needed to go pay this bitch Kia a visit. I couldn't believe she did all of this and ended up in jail.

"Yo you good?" Josh asked.

"Hell, no man the fucking baby is not mine man, he's not mine Josh. This bitch ruined my marriage, my new relationship and I even got attached to the baby and he's not even mine. Before I knew I was crying uncontrollably just like a baby. I was crying about everything all at once; this shit broke a nigga down. Josh got up from his seat and pulled me in for a hug.

"Man, you live, and you learn. I'm not saying that's what you get. I'm just hoping that you've learn from this bullshit. Now get yourself situated and go see his mama and find out who his real daddy is. So, he could be with his rightful family. Josh was right I wiped my eyes and sat at my desk so I could make a couple if phone calls. I even called one of my peeps that worked at the county jail to see if he could get me a visit this evening. Once I was finished making the arrangements, I gathered my things then made my way to Kesha's house.

A half hour later I was knocking on Kesha's door. It took her a little minute to open the door, but she finally did. I could tell that she had been sleeping an I was sorry that I woke her.

"Hey Kesha, can we talk?" I asked with a serious tone. "I thought you had to work today?" She said.

"I did, but I left because I needed to show you this," I said while handing her the DNA paper. After looking over it for a couple of minutes she looked up at me with sad eyes. I didn't need anyone's sympathy because this was my fault. I should have just kept my dick in my pants.

"Oh My God Mark! Come on in." Kesha said while moving to the side. I looked around the house to see where the baby was. and he was lying in his bouncer sound asleep. Kesha had all types of baby stuff around her house as if baby Marquis lived with her.

"I wanted to talk to you about where the baby would go in the event, we can't notify his father."

"To be honest with you Mark. I don't know, I'm not ready to be no one's mother and Kia is not the easiest person to get along with. Then again, I don't wanna see my nephew in the system, so I'm still thinking my decisions through. Of course, I would have to talk it over with my husband. We are just getting back on good terms and doing counseling. I just hope and pray this don't mess up our marriage. Even though I could tell that he's into Marquis and that he would be a big help."

"Well first things first. Let's find out who the daddy of this baby is then we take it from there. After that you could figure out what you wanna do from here on out. I'll be back to pick him up later tonight after I go pay ya sister a visit." I assured Kesha, but I could tell she was in deep thought about something.

"You know what Mark. I'm going to go downtown tomorrow and file for temporary custody until Kia gets out. I'm not sure who this baby daddy is, so I don't wanna be just sending my nephew off with anyone. Can you just do me a favor and let Kesha know for me. I know she's upset because I haven't been to see her or answered any of her calls, but I'm trying to get my life in order, and I can't keep worrying about Kia. She got herself in to shit, and now looked she messed up her life on top of others. I just can't with her."

"I'll deliver the message, but you know you're going to have to speak to her sooner or later." I told Kesha. While standing up and heading out. I needed to get home and get myself in order before I made my way to the jail.

I was currently living in hell. I had been into a couple of fights already and time had been added on to my 10-year sentence. I couldn't believe they gave me this much time for cutting up a dumb bitch. I often cried at night because I was going to miss ten years of my son's life over a nigga that wouldn't even answer my phone calls. The crazy part was I still felt like Mark and I had a chance when I got up out of here. We could still be a happy family especially since I knew he was the one caring for our son. He wouldn't answer my phone calls, and neither would my dumb ass sister, so I had no choice but to reach out to Joe. I knew he would respond. He kept it short and simple though. His bitch ass didn't want his crybaby wife to know he was going behind her back keeping me posted about my son.

"Jones, you have a visitor." The C.O said standing outside my cell.

"If it's not my lawyer I don't want no visitors." I sassed. He looked at me in disgust like he didn't give a damn what I said and still opened the cell. I just rolled my eyes and got up off my bunk. These people in here treated us like animals. I guess this is what I get for being dumb over a nigga.

"How many times I have to tell you, Jones? You don't have a say so in here we own you young lady. If you wanted to be free and run your own life. You shouldn't have done what you did to end up in here. Now let's go I don't have all fucking day." C.O Cleveland snapped. He was a nice-looking older man with salt in pepper hair, but he was just so damn mean. His wife must not have been keeping him happy at home. If I wasn't so up on Mark. I may have shot my shot with his old ass.

Once we made it out of my cell. We made our way to the visiting area. I was shocked to see Mark ass sitting on the other side of the glass window that separated us. I sat in the seat and stared at how handsome he was before I picked the phone up. My man was still looking good like the first day he did when I met him. The only difference was he wasn't wearing a suit. He had on a pair of sweats and knowing him he was probably leaving out of here to go meet up with some bitch. I grabbed the phone one he pointed to it. "Hey baby daddy! It's about time you made time to come up here to see me. Where's our son at?" I asked truthfully wanting to know.

"He's what your sister. I needed to see you I have some important things to discuss with you."

The look on his face looked serious and I wondered what he wanted. I hadn't done shit because I was in here and I hope he didn't think he was getting custody of my damn son. Then again this was my first time seeing him since I sliced up his little girl- friend. Maybe he was still pissed off with me.

"What could you possibly have to discuss with me Mark? If it's about your little girlfriend I don't wanna talk about that. She got what the fuck she deserved for being in my damn way. You knew you had a family to get prepared for, but no you just wanted to parade around the city with ya new bitch." I sassed.

The look on Mark's face showed me that he wasn't pleased at what I said.

"Kia cut the bullshit ma...I should have known from the moment I started fucking with you that you weren't about shit. That fucking whole baby scam was fucked up. You fucked my whole entire family up lying about this baby. I was done with you, been done with you and was trying to get my life back on track. Then you popped up blaming a baby on me that wasn't even mine. When I opened up them fucking papers today. I was hurt, and the only reason I was hurt was because I had gotten so attached to a baby that wasn't mine. When I had to time to go home and think about the shit. Then I got happy that the baby wasn't mine, because that meant I didn't have to deal with ya crazy ass." Mark snapped causing the guards to look at me.

I was glad it wasn't really visiting hours and nobody else was out here. He must have knew people to arrange a meeting like this.

"Mark what the fuck are you talking about? I know who my baby belongs too."

"Yeah whatever you say...I'm about to be out, but the C.O has your copy of the results and your sister told me to let you know; that she'll be going down town in the morning to file for custody of the baby. Which I think will be good since he doesn't need to be raised by an unstable ass bitch like you." Mark started to laugh uncontrollably while walking away.

My blood was boiling, if I wasn't in here, I would have killed his ass for sure. The C.O walked me to my cell and as soon as we made it, he handed me the letter. I sat on the bed in deep thought before I opened the letter. I knew Mark wasn't lying to me, but I knew there was nothing left for me to say to him. I knew one thing for sure I knew exactly who my baby daddy was, but I was taking this shit to my grave it was no way I could let this get out. I closed the letter up and laid down on my bunk. The tears started to run down my face, I was so hurt that the man I loved was never going to talk to me ever again.

———

IT WAS ABOUT TWELVE IN THE AFTERNOON AND IT WAS TIME FOR

my phone call. I couldn't wait to talk to my sister. I don't know who the fuck told her she could go file for custody of my damn son. She had no fucking right; the bitch won't even contact me or answer my calls. The CO came and got me and my cellmate from our cell. My cellmate wasn't going she had given me her call. Of course, I had to give her something in return. I was happy though because I had so much to talk about and I needed more than fifteen damn minutes.

Once I got to the phone, I was happy no one else was standing there. I hurried and dialed my sisters' number. I was praying that she didn't hang up because I needed to get this shit off my chest. To my surprise she excepted the collect call and said hello.

"I knew you would be calling. Mark must have delivered my message."

"Yes, he did, and I don't know why the fuck you thought it would be a good idea to take my son. You're only supposed to be just keeping him while I'm in here not forever Kesha. If you want a baby go have one of your own."

The line had gotten quiet and I knew it was because her bitch ass was about to start crying. See Kesha couldn't have kids. Yup...I had trouble holding them and she straight out couldn't have any. I felt bad about her situation, but that didn't mean she could have my kid.

"First of all, I don't want your baby Kia, and the nerve of you talking to me like this. When I have the upper hand in this situation. If I wanted your baby, I'm sure I could get him, because from my understanding he doesn't have a daddy and I'm his next of kin unless you want him in the system. I'll be sure to let him go then you won't never see him again. As a matter of fact, I think I'll do that since you wanna be a bitch about the situation."

"Kesha, you wouldn't dare do that shit to me. Plus, he has a daddy, and I'll be sure to tell him."

"Well who is his daddy so I can reach out to him. I'm sure he's somebody else's husband?"

I swear Kesha always rubbed me the wrong way. She stayed judging me and I couldn't stand the shit. I knew she was sitting back having a ball about me being in here. In her eyes I was always a fuck up and she was always doing better than me. Her and Joe were back together living happily ever after and I was in here with no man and no baby. All types of shit was coming to my mind and right then and there I had to let it off my chest. I had to put her in her place. If I wasn't living happily ever after, then no one would.

"You know what Kesha; he does belong to somebody else's' husband. He belongs to your husband. Now go ahead and let his daddy know so that way he could go ahead and file for custody." I snapped while hanging the phone up.

I know what y'all thinking and I don't care. Joe and I slipped up one time and I got pregnant. I knew if he wasn't Mark's that he was Joe's. If Kesha hadn't been a smart ass, she would have never found out like that. My life was fucked up and now so was everyone else's.

O ne year later...
      Zyla
      "Hello Ms. Davis...we just received another shipment."

"Alright Terry...just tag the box and when Jax comes in I'll have him check it out."

"Jax and I were the owners of four furniture stores. Two in Jersey and the other two in Philadelphia. Business was doing amazing and I couldn't be more happier. When Jax and I talked about what type of business he wanted to open when I graduated, I was shocked. Yeah people always purchase furniture it was defi-nitely a good investment.

"Baby what you doing in here?"

"Nothing just going over a couple newer designs. Terry just came and said another shipment came."

"I know they sent me an email letting me know that the ship-ment was coming earlier then usual. So, what ya pretty ass got planned for us later? I saw you text and got excited. What kind of surprise you got for me? I told you I got everything I needed when you told me you'll be my wife," Jax said while pulling in for a big hug.

I had a candlelight dinner planned for the two of us. I was going to tell him that he was going to be a daddy again. I hated that it happen at the time we were planning our wedding, but God knew what he wanted.

"Don't worry about the surprise just make sure you're there on time," I said while kissing his lips.

"I'll definitely be there on time. Did you need me to get Zoey?" "No...Mark called me he was going to pick her up, since he got off early."

Mark was doing ok, we had along talk a year ago when he found out that the baby wasn't his. I didn't wanna talk to him, but I was glad that I did. That made our relationship a lot better and now we were able to co parent better. The main thing I was concerned about was us being better parents to Zoey. Mark also was now dating, and I thought he would be right back on the scene after the shit with Sasha, but nope he chilled for a good while. Mark was honestly messed up with what down, but it served his ass right. Now I can see the change in him. I just hope he changed his ways when it came to relationships.

"Ok...cool I'm about to go check out these shipments, and I'll see your sexy ass at home," Jax said while kissing my forehead.

I noticed with him that he had been in a better place since he left the streets alone. Him and Sasha were on great terms and doing good co-parenting Jayla. She was going through a little depression mode when the shit wet down with Kia, but I had gone over a couple of times and talked to her. After her surgery she started counseling sessions and now she is doing wonderful. She had even met her a new man and he was a good one too. Everyone was definitely doing good even my daddy and Jax grand mom. Daddy was back to work and back on the dating scene, while grandma was still being wined and dined by her companion that we met when she was in the hospital a year ago. Tasia and Khi had been kicking it heavy too. Not too long-ago life was crazy, and I didn't think it was going to get any better until Jax came along and I confessed my love to a hustler.

Jaxen

When I pulled up to the house, I noticed everybody's cars were out front. I was wondering what the hell Zyla had up her sleeve today. Whatever this surprise was it must have been impor- tant for everyone to be invited. Hell...I even saw Sasha's car out front. Some- times it was weird to me how close they had gotten, but then again it made life easier. It definitely made Jayla happy because she often said she had two mamas.

"Yo, bro..." Khi yelled while hopping out of his truck. I looked to the side of him and saw Tasia. I should have known she was going to be with him since they had been joined at the hip lately.

"Hey y'all what's good? What this girl got going on?" I asked looking at Tasia.

"Nope...you won't get me to snitch on my Bff. Babe...I'm going inside, I'll see you when you come in." Tasia said while standing on her tippy toes to kiss Khi.

Once she made her way into the house. I looked at Khi dead in the face trying to get him to tell me what he knew. He raised his hands up as if was surrendering and I just chuckled. We both made our way into the house and like I thought everyone was in atten- dance. Which made me wonder even more what was really going on.

After everyone was in attendance, Zyla grabbed my hand and walked me into the room where everyone was. I sat down on the couch and she sat down on my lap.

"Hello everyone, I know you all are wondering why I called you over here. I needed to share something very special with all of you. I haven't told my fiancé yet, so I figured I might as well tell everyone together." Zyla got up and turned her attention to me. she was now standing, and I was sitting so she was standing in between my legs looking down at me.

"You good baby?" I asked because I saw her eyes starting to water.

"Baby I am more then good. You came right in and swept me off my feet and I'm so grateful for you. When you told me that you were going to show me how I'm supposed to be loved, I don't know why I doubted you, but I did. But baby you came in and showed the hell out and I can't wait for the day to come when I'll be Mrs. Jaxen Taylor. When you asked me to marry you? I thought that was the happiest day of my life, but then a couple weeks ago I was told I was going to be a mother again. I was filled with so much excitement, not only am I about to be your wife but shortly after I will be the mother of your second child. Jaxen Taylor, I love you baby and I can't wait to spend the rest of my life with you."

Zyla had a real nigga sitting here with tears in my eyes. All the relationships I had been in. I never had a woman confess her love to me in front of all our loved ones. So, this meant a lot to me. Zyla was what I had been looking for to make my life complete and now that I had her I was going nowhere. We were growing old and happy together.

Mark

I thought that hearing about Zyla's engagement and baby on the way would have me feeling some type of way, but nope I was actually happy for her. She was happy and I could see it all in her face, besides it was my loss. I treated her terrible for years and now she's finally being loved the way she needed to be loved. My life was finally getting back in order. I had gone through a little depression episode, but I finally worked it out and now I'm back to work. I even go to visit Marquis sometimes even though he wasn't mine I had gotten close to him, so I wanted to continue to see him.

As far as Kesha she ended up getting full custody of Marquis since Kia had caught a murder charge in jail. She had started a relationship with one of the C.O's and when she found out that he was sleeping with another inmate she shanked her. I Kia will never learn her lesson. Kesha and Joe are still together and doing marriage counseling and raising Marquis as their own.

"You alright Mark? You got kind of quiet." Megan asked.

"I'm good baby girl. Just was thinking about a couple of things."

Megan and I were friends we had met at the library. I was doing some research on one of the ball players that my company was trying to do an endorsement with. She was beautiful and I was scared of fucking up, so I told her I wanted us to move slow and see where it goes from there. I knew I had learned my lesson when it took me six months to even give anyone my number. That was definitely a change for me, and I think I'm kind of enjoying the new man that I have become. My past was a lesson learned and for now on I've learned karma is a bad bitch and she definitely comes to collect.

Sasha

Life was great I had gotten my surgery thanks to Jax. At first, I was still feeling some type of way because I was lonely, but I quickly push that shit to the back of my head whenever I think back to the day Kia did this to me. Mark still tried to reach out, but I wouldn't give him the time of day. When I said I was finished with him I was finished. Til' this day I was still pissed because of the situation that went down I still have a little bit of trust issues with my new man. I met Gerald going to therapy sessions and he helped me get through so much. When we started dating, I was scared as hell, but Amanda and Zyla got me right. They told me that I couldn't keep letting the shit that Mark did mess with my happiness. I deserved to be happy and so far, Gerald has made me happy.

"You good sweetheart?" Gerald asked while walking into my living room.

"Yes...I'm fine. I just wanted to apologize for the way I acted. I know sometimes work gets in the way and you may get too busy to call."

"You baby...I just need you to understand, that I'm not him. If I didn't wanna be here with you I wouldn't be. I told you when we first started out that u was looking for a wife not a fling. So, give me a chance to do right by you." Gerald said, causing my heart to melt.

"Ok...Gerald I promise I'll do better, but can you promise me that you won't let me run you away. I'm damaged and I'm trying my hardest to let you love me."

"I'm not going nowhere sweetheart. Right here is where I wanna be." Gerald assured me while leaning over to kiss my cheek.

It was no way that I would let my past relationship mess up what I had going on now. He was good to me and good to Jayla him and Jax even got along. Amanda told me I would know when a good man came along. I think I found the love of my life.

The End...